BANEWIND

M.B. CHAPMAN

BANEWIND

M.B. CHAPMAN

Torchflame Books

Durham, NC

For my father, Kenneth W. Chapman, MD.
With love and wonderful memories.
This is for you.

The sanctuary was on the knoll,
Destroyed by years of war.
The building gray, the moon at bay,
The magic here no more.

But yonder down the valley,
A small village was there.
Its residents few, with darkening hue,
For time had been unfair.

And all because of Gresalmur,
A warlock said to be.
His gleaming eyes and vehement lies
Had made the village flee.

For Gresalmur had a Skeleton,
Made from toughest stone,
And occult power and a Prindon flower
Are what held together its bones.

And over time it terrorized,
Led by Gresalmur's hand.
It killed the young, the demons sung
At Gresalmur's strong command.

And once he claimed the village,
In the sanctuary he hid.
Below the earth, with all his worth,
And the Skeleton did his bid.

So few dared pass the village,
With the Skeleton on the prowl.
The people shivered, their lips quivered
When the Skeleton let out its howl.

1

FLAMES

"ARE YOU READY, BLAINE?"

A man stands in the middle of a darkened lab, staring at a metal platform rising from the concrete ground. With dark, beady eyes he looks to the woman who just spoke, before averting his gaze back to the contraption welded to the floor.

"Are you ready?" she repeats.

The large bird skull adorning her head obscures her face.

"Perhaps he's having second thoughts," another woman sneers, from the lab stool she sits on.

Her silver curls cascade past her face, barely allowing her emerald eyes to sparkle through.

"What's wrong, Blaine?" she says. "Is the mighty Magician *afraid?*"

"If you're more confident in this working, Valkryn, then why don't you volunteer to do it yourself?" Blaine continues gazing at the platform, his hands buried deep in the pockets of his orange trench coat. "Of the few occasions I have constructed makeshift portals without connecting to a specific endpoint, the results have been...less than desirable."

"You sent the orphan through without issue last time." Valkryn's black amethyst latex suit squeaks as she crosses her legs. "How do you account for that?"

"Dumb luck." He pulls at his black goatee, the gears in his mind churning. "Perhaps there's a better way."

"I don't have time for any more foolishness," says the woman with the bird skull. "The boy has already informed us that Sadie Hawthorne and Jensen Saint Clair are in town, ready to protect the girl. With every moment we waste, there is less of a chance we can capture her." She points to the platform. "Get on there now, or the only thing going through that portal will be your lifeless body."

Blaine grunts, adjusting the orange, pointed hat atop his head, before stepping onto the metal. His black boots clang, echoing through the room.

"I'm ready," he says.

The woman with the bird skull nods and picks up an octahedral-shaped crystal from the lab bench nearby.

"Do not fail me." She moves forward as her purple cloak glides against the floor. "The girl is the only key we have to breaking the spell."

"If she's even what you say she is," Blaine says.

The woman turns the crystal in her hand, and he vanishes.

"You really think this will work?" Valkryn looks at where Blaine stood just moments before.

"Addisyn DeWinter never told us about the existence of her daughter," says the woman with the bird skull. "The Holy Guardian's bloodline has always been passed on through the female lineage. The next paladin would have to be her."

"But she's not from this world." Valkryn frowns. "She was born outside of Banewind."

"That makes no difference." The woman with the bird skull turns toward the lab's exit. "You cannot escape destiny, Valkryn." She pauses at the door. "I have learned that all too well."

She leaves Valkryn alone, in silence, as she disappears into the darkened corridor.

The evening sky above the forest is splotched with stars, reawakening to blanket the world in their beauty once again. The faint breeze in the midsummer night's air carries with it the woodland's melody—a cacophony of chirping crickets and singing nighthawks. In the trees' hollows, the majestic owls arise from their slumber, ready to cast their watchful gaze over the land. And there, in the center of the forest, stands Blaine.

Alive. Relief washes over his mind.

He looks around at the trees and shrubbery, taking a hesitant step as if testing the muddy ground. When he seems content with his surroundings, he steps through the foliage, pushing the branches and twigs out of his way. Within minutes, he has broken through the forest's edge and finds himself at the top of a hill. From there, he sees the quaint cityscape that lies below, dotted with specks of light from the streetlamps and car headlights that speed through the dark.

Blaine treks down the hill and continues toward the city's outskirts. He finds himself outside of an abandoned church. As he approaches the wooden doors, he sees a plaque adorning the nineteenth-century brick wall, the remnants of its founding date having rusted away with time. A thick metal chain is wrapped around the handles, preventing him from entering.

He clears his throat and grips the padlock in his calloused hands. An orange glow radiates from his fingertips, evolving into flames that dance until they are chewing through the metal lock. The fire reflects off his face, illuminating his worn, pock-marked skin. Soon the metal glows molten red as it melts into a mound of gelatinous goo, dripping through the cracks between his fingers.

Hissssssssssssss! Snap!

The chain unravels through the handles as it clangs to the ground.

He forces open the doors, shielding his face as a thick cloud of dust billows out into the night air. His footsteps echo through the church's vaulted ceilings as he treads across the marble floor with his black boots. He pauses at the altar, slowly turning in a circle to take in his surroundings.

He removes his orange, pointed hat and clutches at its brim, rubbing it between his fingers while grunting.

"Hmm. This could work." He taps his foot against the marble floor. "Yes, this could work."

As he stands there thinking about the project ahead of him, his memory stirs back to the first time he ever created a portal.

"*You're never going to amount to anything, Blaine,*" his father had jeered, taking a hammer to the metal structure he'd worked so hard on. "*The opportunity to study at the Academy, and you waste it on meaningless projects like this? You're no engineer. I'm disappointed to even call you my son.*"

Blaine shakes the image from his head.

If he could only see me now. A sardonic grin spreads across his face. *The feared Magician, chief tinkerer to the Voidweavers' army.*

He pulls out a cell phone and dials a number.

"Hello?" a young man answers.

"I'm here, Scythe. Do you have the girl?"

Outside, a murder of crows soar into the night sky, startled awake by the church bell's thunderous roar resonating from the belfry tower.

2

HELLO, I'M GENEVIEVE

I'M AT THE TOP OF THE MARBLE STAIRCASE. My ballgown rustles around me as I move, the long train cascading behind me like foaming, white waves. As I step down onto the first stair, I grasp the golden handrail with my pearlescent laced glove. The silk is soft against my fingers. My silver heels glitter in the light from the Victorian chandelier, and I know I could put Cinderella to shame right now. The parlor below me is bursting at the seams with thousands of guests, all looking up in a breathless silence. Waiting for me.

And at the bottom of the staircase, there he stands.

I feel myself being drawn to him, entranced by the mystery that shrouds him. He stands still as a statue, dressed in a double-breasted black tuxedo and a silver bow tie that matches the embroidery in my gown. The white mask he wears hides his features. He extends an open hand, beckoning me.

My heart thumps against my ribcage as I descend, bringing me one stair closer to him. But just as I do, another step appears at the bottom of the staircase, and I haven't moved an inch. Panic hits me. I clutch tighter to the railing and hurry down the stairs. Still, the distance between us never decreases.

I run, taking the stairs two at a time now, stumbling over my feet, twisting my ankle in the silver heels. No, this can't be happening. I can see him there, waiting for me, holding out his hand. But I cannot reach him!

The tears well up in my eyes, and I start screaming, "Don't leave me!"

He retracts his hand.

"No, wait! I'm here."

I can't move any faster. The staircase is blurring past me now. The chandelier above me buzzes, hurting my ears as the lightbulbs explode. The room grows dark. The people are disappearing. I can't see him anymore.

And then I wake up.

I roll onto my side and slap the top of my alarm clock, groaning at the realization that I can't even get a man in my own dreams. I take my phone off its charger. No messages. But who has anything to say at six in the morning? Certainly not me. I hate mornings.

I lie in bed for several minutes, trying to find the motivation to get going. The sunlight has already managed to creep past my lavender curtains, brightening my room in a golden hue. It catches on the various posters I have scattered on my pink walls, from Shakespeare surrounded by the leading roles in his plays, to an ensemble of *Harry Potter* characters, all of which helped me escape during the sadder moments in my childhood.

I head into the bathroom and take a shower, letting the warm water wash over my body. I close my eyes as I scrub the shampoo into my hair. The boy from my dream pops into my head, and I realize I don't even know what his face looks like. Every time I try to recall it, I see nothing

7

but the mask he was wearing. It frustrates me more than it should. I mean, it's just a dream. I'm not going to be anyone's Cinderella—not anytime soon, anyway.

"Good morning, Jeannie," my dad says, as I enter the kitchen. "Don't you look cute as a button! Ready for your first day of senior year?"

"As much as I can be." I walk over to the stove to give him a kiss on the cheek.

He's attempting to make scrambled eggs, and seems to be losing the battle.

"But remember, it isn't just any first day. It's my *last* first day. Ever."

"Until you start college." He laughs. "Have you narrowed down your list yet?"

"I dunno." I take some juice from the refrigerator. "I still think Stanford or Vanderbilt would be amazing for journalism. Not sure my ACT scores will hold up for that, though."

"There's nothing wrong with staying local, you know." He smiles. "You have an advantage with your old man here working at Case Western Reserve. I might be a biology professor, but I have plenty of contacts in the English department."

"I know, I know." I laugh. "We'll see. Where's Danny?"

"I think he's still upstairs getting ready. Maybe you should go make sure he's awake."

"I'm here!" my little brother shouts, as he barrels down the stairs.

Seconds later, he slides in from the hallway and plops down at the kitchen table.

"Good morning." He beams as he shoves several folders into his backpack. "What's for breakfast?"

"Eggs and bacon." Dad scoops the eggs onto a plate and drops them in front of Danny, with a glass of milk. "I made them especially for you."

Danny looks at the plate and grimaces. "Oh, thanks, Dad." He hesitates before taking a bite of the eggs, but seems pleased when he does. "Mmm. These are pretty good."

"You should be grateful you don't have to get your own breakfast." I smile. "Most thirteen-year-olds are pretty capable of making their own food."

Danny rolls his eyes. "Whatever, Vee." He scans my outfit. "Did you dress yourself in the dark?"

An ironic comment coming from someone wearing a pair of basketball shorts and an Adidas T-shirt.

"Daniel." My father sits with his own plate of food. "Be nice."

"What?" Danny swallows a gulp of milk. "It looks like she got her clothes from an old ladies store."

"That's not true!" I go into the foyer to look in the antique mirror hanging on the wall.

I'm dressed in a new white blouse and pink hooded sweater, along with a pair of faded capri jeans. My light brown hair falls down my shoulders in wavy curls, and I'm wearing no makeup.

"This is a new outfit, Danny."

"Yeah." He grins. "That you got from the old ladies store."

"Don't tease your sister." Dad ruffles the top of Danny's spiked brown hair. "Remember, she's babysitting you after school today, so you'll be at her mercy."

"Ugh," Danny groans. "Don't use that word. It sounds so childish."

"You *are* a child." I laugh.

It's almost seven-thirty.

"Oh! I gotta go pick up Katie." I grab the car keys off the hook on the wall. "I don't want to be late."

"Be careful driving, honey. I love you."

I walk over and kiss my dad on the top of his head. His graying brown hair seems to be receding faster by the day.

"I'll be working late," he says, "so you may want to get dinner for you two."

"No problem." I turn to kiss my little brother on the cheek. "Have fun today, squirt. Love ya."

He wipes off his cheek. "Gross."

It only takes five minutes to reach Katie's house, so I have to wait before she's ready to go. I know I shouldn't be nervous for school, but as I'm sitting alone in my black Honda Civic, I can feel the butterflies creeping into my stomach. I've done this a dozen times before, but each year brings with it new schedules, new teachers, new challenges, and now a whole new layer of anxiety with college applications. And although I am excited about where my future is taking me, the constant pressure of succeeding and doing the right thing is always there. I mean, *the right thing*. Does that even exist? Who's to say? I know I worry about too much stuff, but it's just a trait that runs in my family. My mother was the absolute worst for it.

"Good morning, Jeannie." Katie opens the passenger side door and flashes a mouthful of braces as she smiles at me. "You ready for our first day of senior year?"

Her strawberry blonde hair is in two braids that fall onto her shoulders, and she's wearing big black-rimmed glasses that make her look adorably geeky. The perfect look you'd expect for someone who will be graduating as our class valedictorian.

"Not really." I laugh. "I could have used a little more of a summer vacation."

"Right? It's crazy how fast the time goes."

"Can you believe it's already been two months since we were in Niagara Falls? Will our families even be able to do trips like that together once we're in college?"

I pull out of the driveway, and nostalgia washes over me as memories of other summer trips flash through my head...especially when I was younger, and my mother was still alive. Her inviting smile and bright blue eyes, that warm and jovial laugh...

"Sure we will!" Katie beams. "We'll still get time off."

"Says the girl planning to go to medical school." I smirk, letting my mom's image flutter away. "I have a feeling your college summers will be tied up with activities."

"Not enough to change our friendship! We're best friends forever, Jeannie. *Forever.*"

"Right." I chuckle as I turn on the radio.

For the remainder of the ride we belt out the lyrics to Halsey's newest single.

When we arrive at school, the campus is already a hive of activity. The parking lot is full. The sidewalks are packed with students running every which way, and a flood of people is pouring into the building. The last of the school buses are arriving now, carrying mostly nervous freshmen that are terrified to step out of the yellow doors.

I smile as I remember how afraid I was on my first day of high school, but then the butterflies in my stomach remind me that little has changed.

"We're in the same homeroom together, right?" Katie pulls out a paper schedule from her skirt's pocket. "Biology? With the new teacher, Miss Hawthorne?"

"Correct." I place a magnetic mirror inside my locker before shutting the door. "It would have been funnier if she taught English."

"What? Why?"

"You know, cause her last name's Hawthorne. Like Nathanial Hawthorne."

"That...is a very lame joke." Katie laughs.

"Yeah, I realized it as I said it." I giggle back.

The warning bell for class rings, and we head off down the hall.

Every seat in the classroom is taken except for the first three desks at the front of the room. I groan as I take my place in the chair, feeling like all eyes are fixed on me. I hate sitting up front. It feels like you're on display.

"Oh, she's so pretty," Katie whispers, as she nods towards the teacher standing at the chalkboard.

She's wearing a periwinkle dress that falls just below her ankles.

The bell rings to start first period.

"Okay, guys, settle down," Miss Hawthorne says in a sweet, melodic voice, wearing a warm, inviting smile. "I hope everyone had a good summer." She walks over to her desk and picks up a piece of paper. "I know for me it went too fast."

Several people laugh in agreement.

"I'm going to run through the attendance before we get started with introductions." She pulls a pair of reading glasses off the top of her dark blonde hair and sets them on her nose. "And then I thought we could do a couple ice breakers to get to know each other. So it'll be a pretty easy first day, all right? Let's see..."

Miss Hawthorne begins roll call, stopping after each student acknowledges his or her name so she can ask questions like, *What did you do for the summer?* and *What year are you in school?* I pick up my pen and start scribbling in my notebook, waiting for her to call me.

> *As summer lies her head to sleep,*
> *She tries to block her children's weep.*
> *For school days are here again,*
> *And autumn soon stirs from her den.*

"Genevieve DeWinter?"

I'm startled by the sound of my name, lost in my own poetic thoughts. I put down my pen and raise my hand.

"Here," I say.

Miss Hawthorne smiles at me and nods. "Right up front. I like that." She checks off my name. "Let's see...next we have—"

The classroom door swings open.

He walks in.

My jaw falls to the floor.

"Sorry to interrupt." The boy pulls the door shut behind him. "Is this Miss Hawthorne's class?"

Miss Hawthorne nods. "Yes, that's me." Her laugh sounds like little bells chiming. "Will you be joining us?"

"Yeah." He walks over and hands her a piece of paper. "I just transferred here today."

Miss Hawthorne takes the paper and reads it. She turns to the class as another smile broadens across her face.

"Well, why don't we all give a warm welcome to Jensen Saint Clair."

Jensen raises his hand and gives a slight wave. I catch his eye, but look back down at my scribbled words. The butterflies in my stomach have intensified a thousand-fold.

Oh. My. God.

3

BLUSH

BREATHE. JUST BREATHE, GENEVIEVE. Don't pay any attention to the drop-dead gorgeous boy that just walked into the room. Focus on something else. Think of something else. Just think—

Who am I kidding? I can't. Right now, the only thing my mind cares about is that this boy is the most attractive human I have ever seen. His tanned skin glows with a brilliant radiance, and his short, light brown hair complements his eyes. His lips are red and vibrant, as if they were crafted onto his face, and his jaw line is sharp and defined. His neck is slender, but obviously strong. I can see the outline of his muscles beneath his skin, and I follow them down until they disappear under his gray V-neck shirt.

"He's a cutie, isn't he?" Katie whispers, as she leans over to me. "I think every girl in this room's blushing—maybe even a few of the guys."

"Yeah, he's handsome," I whisper. "And he's probably a complete jerk."

Katie giggles. "You're just trying to find an excuse not to like him."

"No." *Yes.*

"You've joined us at the perfect time, Mister Saint Clair," says Miss Hawthorne. "We were just about to do introductions after I finish up with roll call."

Jensen scans the room with his dark brown eyes. I'm trying to examine him without making it seem too obvious. I'm shielding my eyes with my hand on my forehead, and glancing up just enough to catch a glimpse of him.

You must look absolutely ridiculous. Stop acting crazy.

"Why don't you take a seat?" Miss Hawthorne points him towards an empty desk.

Wait. The empty desk is...it's next to me!

Jensen nods and walks over. He drops his backpack to the side of the desk and slides into his seat, then turns to face my direction.

"Hey there," he whispers, smiling at me with dazzling white teeth.

"I'm, uh, I'm Genevieve." I pick up my pen and pretend to write something down.

I can see him smirking as he pulls out his own notebook.

I sit awkwardly, trying not to stare at him anymore than I already have, as Miss Hawthorne finishes the class roster.

"Okay, everyone. Why don't you pair up with someone you don't know, and introduce yourselves?" Miss Hawthorne claps and looks at me. "Miss DeWinter, correct? Would you mind working with our new classmate?"

"Um, sure."

I try to control my breathing. *Stop acting like an idiot. He's just a new student. Sure, he's good-looking, but that doesn't define him. Appearance isn't the measure of a person.*

But he *must* be an exception to that adage.

Now that he's sitting mere inches away from me, his

sweet cologne wafts in my direction. As he reaches into his backpack, his biceps quiver.

I feel my stomach tie into a tighter knot.

Ugh, Genevieve...stop.

"So," Jensen scoots his desk closer to mine, "Genevieve."

If voices were fabric, his would be softer than silk.

"Hi," I mutter.

He laughs. "What year are you?"

"I'm a senior. What about you?"

"Same. My family just moved here." He frowns. "Still getting settled in."

"Well, I think you'll fit in just fine," I murmur.

"What?"

My face flushes. "Oh, nothing. I just mean...well, I'm sure you'll make lots of friends here."

"Oh." He pauses, but then looks at me and smiles. "Hopefully."

"Okay, so where are you from? Why did you move here?"

"Father's work." He sighs. "We move around quite a bit."

He speaks formally, his tone one I'm not used to hearing with my other friends.

"I'm sorry. I can't imagine moving all the time. It must be awful to have no sense of what a secure home is like." I see Jensen staring at me. "Oh, gosh, I'm sorry. I didn't mean to sound rude or anything."

Did I seriously just tell him how awful his life must be without having a place to call home?

"It's okay. You're fine." A smile is still on his face. "I'm guessing you've never lived anywhere else?"

I shake my head. "No, I haven't. And although the prospect of going to college excites me, I'm trying to block out that I'd be leaving the one place I've come to know and love—good, old Parma, Ohio." I laugh. "Maybe it sounds silly. I don't know." I bite my lip. "So do you have a big family?"

"I have my mom and dad, older sister, older brother, and a younger brother."

"I have a younger brother, too! How old is he?"

"Thirteen."

"So is mine!" I act as if this were the rarest artifact ever to be discovered. "They should meet each other. Danny could always use some more friends."

"Yeah, sure," Jensen says.

I can't tell if he's just being polite.

"What about you?" he says.

"What about me?"

"Your family. You have a younger brother. Anyone else?"

"Just my dad." I hesitate. "My mom died ten years ago."

"Oh, I'm sorry to hear that," he says, and I can see genuine empathy in his eyes. "You must miss her."

"Yes, I do," I whisper.

It's hard to believe she's been gone for so long.

Okay. So he's not a jerk at all. But he must have a flaw. No one's perfect.

"Do you have a favorite thing to do?" He looks at my backpack, with a smirk. "I see you have several novels in there."

I look down into the unzipped section and see my copies of *Cloud Chamber*, *Things Fall Apart*, and *The Great Gatsby*.

"Yeah, I love reading." I pull out one of the novels and flip it around.

The feel of a book is always comforting to me.

"And writing, actually," I say. "I'm planning to do something with that in college. Maybe journalism or English."

"Oh, that's awesome. What do you like to write?"

"Anything." I laugh. "Poetry, short stories…whatever, really. I'm president of the Creative Writing Club. And I help out on the school newspaper."

He grins. "You're very cute."

"Ha, thanks." I blush, unsure if he's teasing me. "What about you?"

"I enjoy running."

"Oh, yeah? My best friend is on the track team." I gesture to Katie sitting next to me. "Do you do cross country or track?"

"What do you mean?" He gives me a strange look.

"Oh, I just assumed you ran in school."

He still doesn't seem to understand what I'm asking.

"Exercise really isn't my thing," I say, after another moment. "I definitely got more of my father's brains than my mother's brawn. She was always doing things like skiing, climbing, and hiking. Although, she was just as smart, to be honest."

"Sounds like a great family," he says, in a warm tone.

I feel a hand on my shoulder and turn to see Katie smiling at us.

"Mind if I butt in?"

"Not at all." I'm grateful for her coming to the rescue, as I felt like I was running out of things to talk to him about. "Jensen, this is Katie."

"Hey there. Nice to meet you." He waves. "So you

BANEWIND

two have been friends for a while, then?"

"Since birth." Katie giggles.

I roll my eyes and laugh. "What Katie means is that both of our moms had us in the hospital at the same time."

"That's right," she says. "Birthday twins. So May thirty-first is kind of a big deal around here."

"Okay, class, why don't we pause the discussions for a bit and start going over the syllabus." Miss Hawthorne passes out stacks of paper. "There'll be plenty of time to get to know each other better."

"When do you have lunch?" Jensen grabs the syllabus from Miss Hawthorne.

"Fifth period," I say. "You?"

"Same." He smiles. "Maybe we can continue this conversation then?"

"Sounds good to me."

I glance at Katie and have to bite my lip to keep from smiling too hard as I see her give me a thumbs up.

Good-looking, athletic, and nice. I glance at Jensen. *And I thought guys like that didn't exist in our world.*

The rest of my morning classes pass by in a blur, and finally lunch period rolls around. I head into the cafeteria and buy my lunch, looking to see if any of my friends are already seated. Sure enough, I spot Katie sitting at a table in the back corner.

"Hey, Genevieve," a voice calls, from behind me.

Without skipping a beat, my heart flutters into my throat, and I know who it is before the final syllable of my name even hits my ears. I turn around, and Jensen is standing just inches away from me. He has his backpack slung over one shoulder and is carrying his food tray.

"Hey." I try to sound calm. "How are you?"

"Starving." He flashes his white teeth. "Mind if I join you for lunch?"

"Not at all."

We head over to the table.

"Hey, Jeannie." Katie waves at me.

She sees Jensen walking beside me and her face brightens.

"Oh, hey, Jensen."

I take a seat next to Katie, and Jensen sits on the other side of me.

"So how were the rest of your mornings?" I say. "Any first-day drama?"

"Hardly." Katie sighs. "I'm starting to regret signing up for so many AP classes. But Jensen and I are in AP physics together. We chose each other as lab partners."

"Ah, well, you picked a good one, Jensen." I laugh. "Katie is extremely smart."

"Yeah, I caught on to that quickly." He grins.

"So is he!" Katie says. "We geeked out over our mutual love for chemistry. I think I may have recruited a new body for the Chem Club. Did you know he did an internship last summer at the NIH, with biomedical engineering?"

"Wow, that's impressive." I open my Coke Zero. "So you're a genius, too."

"I wouldn't say that." Jensen chuckles, rubbing the back of his head.

It's cute to see him acting so modest.

"How did you end up getting that position?" I say.

"My father knows a lot of people, so that helped."

"What does he do?" Katie says.

"He works in politics and government stuff. You know, it's complicated and boring."

"Um, not boring," Katie says. "Fun fact—my dad is the superintendent for this school district."

"What she's trying to say is that there's nothing her family can't do." I giggle. "I'm lucky to have her as a friend."

"Aww, well I can say the same." Katie rests her head on my shoulder. "Genevieve is like the sister I never had."

"To which I reply, she's more than welcome to take my brother for as long as she wants if she's looking for a sibling."

"Hey, I've grown used to the only-child life. I can't complain."

"Katie?"

A tall, lanky boy with glasses thicker than Katie's is standing next to us, holding his lunch tray. His shaggy blonde hair sits on his head, curling at its edges. His *Legend of Zelda* T-shirt is a size too big for his skinny frame, but his jeans are too short for his height, exposing several inches of his pale ankles, a stark contrast to the bright red Converse he wears.

"Floyd!" Katie flushes. "Hey, what's up?"

"Not too much. Just got done with choir practice." He pauses. "Can I join you guys for lunch?"

"Sure!" She pulls over her sandwich to make more room for him.

"Hi, Floyd," I say.

"Hiya, Genevieve." As he sits, he knocks over his water bottle, but picks it up before too much spills. "Oh, shoot!"

"Here." Jensen uses a napkin to clean up the spilled water. "I got it."

"Thanks," Floyd grins, his cheeks turning red. "I'm rather clumsy."

"It's fine. I'm Jensen, by the way."

Floyd nods. "Nice to meet you."

"So how's your first day?" Katie says.

I always love how awkward the two of them are together. They've had a thing for each other over the last couple years, but still haven't officially started dating.

"It's been pretty good." His eyes brighten. "You're in BC calculus with me this afternoon, right?"

"Yeah, that's right. I'm excited." Katies blushes. "I mean, I think it's gonna be a good class."

Jensen and I exchange smirks.

"Well, I wanted to talk to you about something." Floyd adjusts his glasses. "I was thinking that maybe on Friday we could go see a movie together...if you'd like."

"Oh! That sounds like fun." Katie turns to me, clearly signaling with her eyes for me to intervene.

She always gets so nervous at the idea of being alone with Floyd.

"Could Genevieve tag along? I already told her we could hang out this weekend."

This girl is such a bad liar.

"Oh, yeah, sure. I'd be happy to see a movie. Would you like to come with us?" I turn to Jensen, my heart racing as I wait for his reply.

"Yeah, that'd be great."

I can't contain the smile that spreads across my face.

"Oh...okay, yeah," Floyd says. "I mean, I thought maybe it could just be you and me. But, um, yeah, that would be fun. I'll look forward to it."

"Are you going to do Book Club again this year with me?" I say. "I'm hoping we can get some more recruits."

"Duh." Floyd laughs. "I already have several novels picked out."

"What are you reading now?"

"I finally started *A Game of Thrones*. I had to get on the bandwagon."

I laugh. "Well, I beat you to it. I fell in love with the series a couple years ago. It's completely different from the show."

Floyd's cell phone buzzes from his pocket.

"Oh, crap!" He jumps up from the table. "I forgot the robotics team was meeting now. I have to get going. I'm sorry." He turns to Katie. "I'll see you in math."

"Likewise," she says, as he rushes off.

"Likewise?" I giggle. "What kind of a reply is that?"

"Gah, Jeannie! I don't know." She clasps her hands to her head. "You know I always get all flustered when Floyd's around."

"I don't understand why you guys aren't dating yet. You're perfect for each other."

"I'm just going to wait for him to make the first move," Katie says, her eyes downcast.

"Uh, I know I don't know you guys that well, but I'm pretty sure trying to get you to go to the movies with him alone was a move in itself." Jensen laughs. "Although, I'm more than happy to go on a double date."

"Date?" My stomach ties into knots. *Did he just say this was a date?*

"Whatever you want to call it." He grins. "It'll be fun, regardless."

The warning bell sounds for our next class, and all I can think about is that at the end of the week, I'll be spending my Friday night with Jensen Saint Clair.

Jensen.

Oh, the sound of his name...

4

INTO THE WOODS

THE REST OF THE DAY DRAWS ON monotonously as I get through the remaining classes. But Jensen and I did exchange numbers before leaving school, which I consider to be a goal achieved in itself.

I meet Katie back at my car and drop her off at home. I get back to my house at about 3:30, and find Danny already back from school. He's sitting in the family room, with the TV on and his math textbook splayed across the floor in front of him.

"Hey, squirt." I take off my backpack. "How was your first day?"

"Boring." He keeps his gaze glued to the television.

"That's it? Boring? Nothing else?"

"Nah."

A commercial comes on, and he finally finds this reason enough to look at me.

"Now that you're home, I'm going to go over Nick's house. I'll be back in time for dinner." He pulls open the kitchen door. "I was hoping maybe you could go next door and let the dog out for me. Pleeeeeease?"

I scoff at him. "What? Absolutely not. *You're* the one

who said you'd dog sit for them on Wednesdays. Don't pull me into this."

Feeding and walking our neighbor's dog, Grendel, used to be my job on Wednesday afternoons. I passed on that torch to Danny several years ago, when he was old enough to start wanting money.

"Oh, come on, Vee. Please? I'll do something nice for you."

"Like what?"

"Um." He squints while he's thinking. "I'll wash your car this week."

I sigh.

"Please?"

"Okay, fine. But you have to be back by dinner—"

The door slams, and he's gone.

I consider making myself a snack, but decide against it. If I'm going to have to go take care of the dog, I might as well do it now before I settle in for the evening.

I grab their house keys from the decorative blue bowl on the foyer table, and head out the front door. As I'm walking down the driveway, my phone vibrates in my pocket and my pulse starts racing.

Maybe it's Jensen. I pull out my phone so it's face down.

After I take a deep breath, I flip it around and see that it's only an email notification.

I sigh and drop the phone back into my jeans.

Calm down. Just calm down.

I use the keypad to enter in through the garage, and the minute I jingle the key I can hear the ferocious beast scratching on the other side of the door. Once the garage door is back down, I clutch the knob and swing it open. The dog nearly knocks me down the stairs.

"Whoa, Whoa! Relax." I stumble backwards as the one-hundred-fifty-pound Great Dane barrels into my chest.

"I said relax, Grendel!"

His tongue laps against my face several times—warm, wet, and slimy.

"Ugh, you're so gross." I laugh, pushing him down off of me and rubbing the side of his Harlequin coat.

He falls to the cement floor and rolls onto his back, signaling me to scratch his stomach. I bend down and greet him for a couple more minutes, before entering the house to get his leash and harness.

After he's hooked up, we're back outside and walking down the sidewalk. Well, he's tugging my arm out of its socket, and I'm just following where he wants to go. But I don't really care. I gave up a long time ago trying to control him. I'd have better luck training a wolf.

The street is quiet this afternoon, and a slight wind is blowing through the fading summer's day. The sun shines above me, and several bird silhouettes can be seen swooping back and forth in the sky, looking for prey in the nearby woods. An elderly man is reading a novel on his porch swing while his wife digs in the garden below him. I smile at the picturesque scene.

And then I'm tumbling.

I'm not sure what happened, but my feet give out beneath me. As they swing forward into the air, I plummet backwards to the sidewalk and hit the concrete with a *thud!* The breath is knocked out of my lungs, and I lie there, dazed. My hands are resting next to me, and I feel as though I'm on something cold. Not just cold, but *freezing* cold. Did I slip on...on ice? No, that's impossible.

I look down and see a glistening layer of ice resting

beneath my body. It's already started melting in the sun's heat, but there is no doubt that the frozen sidewalk is the cause of my fall.

"What?"

My jeans are damp, and I wipe my wet hands on them before sitting up. I look around and see the elderly couple working on their activities, failing to notice that I just nearly cracked my back in half.

Wait. Something's not right.

Oh! Grendel!

I'm back up on my feet and scanning the area, looking for the loose dog. On the other side of the street, Grendel's darting towards the woods, barking at a squirrel. He's moments away from disappearing into the trees.

"Oh, crap! Grendel! Grendel! Come here, boy."

Of course, he doesn't even acknowledge me. Stupid dog.

"Grendel, come. Grendel!" I shout, knowing my cries are futile.

As I bound across the street, he stops and sits, cocking his head as he stares at me with his big, dopey face.

"Grendel." I pant, leaning over to catch my breath.

I'm standing on the sidewalk and can see the leash trailing just a couple feet in front of me.

"Good boy," I coo, inching forward. "That's a good boy. Stay."

A nearby branch falls to the ground, and he shoots off into the woods.

"Damn it!" I rush forward and push the branches and twigs away with my hands, trying to shield my eyes as I enter the forest.

The sun fades until all that lights the forest is a dim, gray hue.

"Grendel," I bark a whisper.

I'm being coaxed deeper and deeper into the woods, and all I can think about are the vast majority of horror movies I've watched where this same situation played out and didn't end so well.

"I'm going to kill you, stupid mutt," I hiss, avoiding a decaying log on the ground.

The fallen leaves crunch beneath my feet, and the sweet forest's scent fills my nostrils.

After another five minutes, I break through more shrubbery and find myself in a small, circular clearing. Most of the trees are dead, and having fallen over, they leave only scattered stumps as proof of their once existence.

Feeling defeated, I let out a long sigh as I sit on one of the stumps.

"Great." I kick a stone near my foot. "Just great."

"Are you looking for something?" a voice echoes across the trees.

I jump to my feet and gasp as I turn to see a boy standing at the clearing's other side. He's leaning against a dying tree.

My sympathetic nervous system kicks in as my body prepares for fight or flight. The boy *looks* harmless—he seems to be about my age—but then again, he's obscured by the shadows and it's hard for me to fully judge.

"I can't find my dog," I whisper, after deciding it doesn't matter what I do.

If he wanted to hurt me right now, telling him about Grendel isn't going to change that.

"The Great Dane?" He steps forward from the darkness. "I saw him run off that way a little bit ago." He gestures behind me.

I don't turn around to look.

Now that he's in better light, I can get a good view of him. I'm right on the age part—he's probably eighteen or nineteen—and he's very attractive. He has black hair that swoops over the side of his forehead, and blue eyes that are sparkling like sapphires. His face is beautiful, with high-set cheekbones and a slender nose. His skin is pale and ashen, but it suits him well. And his body appears fit beneath the turquoise track jacket and matching track pants he wears.

"Want me to help you look for him?" He takes another step toward me.

"It's okay. Thanks." I back up. "You don't have to do that."

"I don't mind." He stares at me with a wolfish grin, and I feel as though his blue eyes are piercing through my body. "It really isn't smart for you to be out here alone."

"What about you?" I snap back. "I mean, really. A girl can't spend her time alone in the woods, but it's perfectly acceptable for a boy?"

His eyes widen in surprise. "I-I guess you make a good point." He bites his lips.

They have a blue tint to them.

"What's your name?"

"Genevieve." *Can he tell I'm caught off-guard?*

"I'm Scythe. Nice to meet you."

We both stand there in awkward silence.

"Okay. Well, I'm going to go find my dog. Take care."

"Wait." He jerks his hand towards me. "Why don't you stay here, and I'll go find the dog and bring him back to you." He looks proud of himself for suggesting this. "If not, you might get lost."

"These woods aren't that big. I'll be fine." I'm beginning to get agitated with this punk. "I appreciate you offering to help. But seriously, I'm just going to—"

The tree behind Scythe explodes into thousands of splinters, crackling while the red blaze ascends to the top. As I fall to the ground, I see him bound to the left and roll behind a hollowed trunk, taking cover from the hissing flames. The clearing illuminates with a fiery orange light as the trunk bursts into dancing embers.

I cover my eyes, blinded by the fire's brightness as it continues to engulf the shrubbery around me. My face is drenched in sweat, and my breathing is swift and shallow. Up and down, up and down, up and down. My chest rises and falls so fast I'm afraid I'll pass out if I don't get myself under control.

Another explosion.

I cover my ears and scream.

I drag myself over to a stump and hide behind it, scanning the clearing to see what has become of the boy. About twenty feet from me, his body lies sprawled out, with flames flickering just inches from his clothes. A nearby tree explodes and falls to the ground, revealing a figure in a hooded red cloak standing in its place.

He slowly approaches the motionless boy.

"Scythe! Look out!" I scream, on the verge of tears.

The cloaked figure snaps his head in my direction. Scythe jumps to his feet and throws his arm out in front of him. A blinding, blue bolt surges from his hand and crashes into the hooded figure's chest. The figure tumbles through the air like a rag doll and crashes into a tree, snapping the trunk in two, and plummets to the ground.

My jaw falls open as I watch Scythe grab the lowest hanging branch and pull himself into the treetop's canopy with the finesse of a jungle creature. The hooded figure stirs on the ground and sits up, shaking off his injuries.

I hear high-pitched whistling coming from above,

and seconds later a barrage of white shards is descending into the clearing like guided missiles. A gust of icy air hits my face.

The hooded figure looks to my direction. "Run!"

As the shards approach, he braces himself in a defensive stance and becomes engulfed by a giant sphere of flames. The shards collide with the massive fireball and shatter, scattering their remains around the destroyed clearing like shimmering glitters of winter's snow.

I take off running through the woods. The trees blur by my side, and branches lash out at my skin like tiny daggers. I'm gasping for air, but won't take the risk of stopping. My lungs are on fire, and they scream out in retaliation as they tighten with every step. My vision is hazy, but I can see the forest around me ablaze with the dazzling hues of orange, blue, and white. I don't know if anyone is coming after me. I don't even know what's going on. This must be a dream. This isn't *real*.

I don't know how long I've been running, but I can't go much further. I slow my pace and bend forward, clutching at my stomach as I cough violently, feeling my insides lurch. I'm sweating profusely, and my disheveled hair is sticking to my face. The pink sweater I have on is shredded to pieces, and my arms are covered with soot and ash.

A twig snaps behind me.

I sprint through the woods again. The wind rips at my face, and I can hear the sound of someone chasing after me, gaining distance. I scream, prohibiting my body from giving in. With whatever energy I can muster, I have to escape these woods.

"Hey, stop!" The words rush by me like thunder. "Stop!"

I glance back and see the person in the red cloak.

Focus, Genevieve. Focus.

"Please! Stop!"

No, Genevieve! Don't stop!

"Genevieve, stop!"

I stumble. My mind is racing.

He knows your name?

I don't understand.

A heat swell washes over my body, and the tree in front of me bursts into towering flames. It falls to the forest floor and blocks my path. I skid to a halt.

"Genevieve—"

"Don't come near me!" I back against a tree.

The cloaked figure is mere feet from me.

"Stay away!"

He steps forward and pulls back his hood, letting it fall to his shoulders.

"Genevieve." Jensen keeps his brown-eyed gaze locked on me.

"J-Jensen?" I watch the wind ruffle his cloak.

I feel queasy and fall to my knees, catching the ground with my hands.

"I don't...I don't..."

My vision tunnels. My hearing fades to nothing. I feel myself slipping away from reality...

And then I'm greeted by darkness.

5

ORDERS

SCYTHE ENTERS THE CHURCH and sees the Magician in his orange trench coat, sitting at the front. As he walks down the aisle, he considers turning back, but knows he would be dead before reaching the door. With one last deep breath, he stops next to the pew and waits for the Magician to notice him.

"Are you religious?" The Magician flips through an old Missalette he found lying torn on the floor.

Scythes looks at the orange, pointed hat resting next to him.

He shrugs. "No, not really."

"So if I killed you right now," the Magician discards the text as he turns to glare at Scythe, "you think that would just be it? Nothing more to come?"

Scythe stands in silence.

"*Because I could not stop for Death, He kindly stopped for me,*" the Magician says. "Have you heard that before?"

Scythe shakes his head.

"Of course not. Orphans are never properly educated." The Magician clasps his hands into his lap. "Now tell me...why haven't you gotten the girl?"

"It's not that easy," Scythe snaps. "Jensen Saint Clair showed up and nearly killed me. And Sadie Hawthorne is here now, too. "

"Oh, Scythe." The Magician snorts. "You really expect me to believe that?" He shakes his head. "Come on. You've been here now on your own for several months, following her, learning her schedule, studying her every move. You've had plenty of time, even before their recent arrival."

Scythe says nothing.

The Magician sighs. "Look," he places his hat back on his head as he stands, "I get it. She's a girl. You're a guy. Feelings, emotions, urges." He slaps Scythe's shoulder. "It's all normal. I, too, loved a woman once. But it only ever ends in heartbreak."

"I don't know what—"

"I told Valkryn it was a bad idea to recruit your help. But she insisted that someone Genevieve's own age would make this easier." He shakes his head. "Of course, it's only complicated things."

"Sorry..." Scythe mutters.

The Magician stares at him until Scythe shifts on his feet.

He pats Scythe's shoulder once more and brushes past him.

"Get the girl before we do," the Magician calls, as he nears the church's exit. "Or I will kill you."

Scythe lets out a long sigh as he collapses onto the church's pew and buries his face in his hands. From the moment he became an orphan at the age of ten, his life had been nothing but miserable. No memories of his parents, no memories of his childhood, no memories of... happiness. All he has known are the cold, sterile walls of the Orphanotrophium, the harsh punishments dealt out by the Voidweaver soldiers, and the constant angst of feeling that at any moment his life was dispensable, like a quick puff of air extinguishing a candle—no existence to be remembered.

He recalls the words the Magician just spoke. *Because I could not stop for Death, He kindly stopped for me.*

As Scythe sits there in the church's stale air, he can't help but wonder, *Maybe it would be better to stop for Death.*

Maybe that's the best he can hope for.

6

THE FORMULISTS

"*I STILL CAN'T BELIEVE THIS.*"

"It was going to happen eventually."

"Yes, Jensen. *Eventually*. Not now."

"What did you want me to do? Risk letting her stay there with Scythe? He could have killed her."

"What you *should* have done was made sure Scythe never approached her in the first place. You let your guard down."

"Oh, I'm sorry, Sadie. Next time, I just won't answer when Thaddeus Loring calls. That'll go over well, right?"

"I don't appreciate your sarcasm."

"I don't appreciate you acting like this is all *my* fault."

"You're supposed to be protecting her, Jensen. Start acting like it."

I've been awake for several minutes now, keeping my eyes closed as I listen to the two of them bickering. I recognize Jensen's voice, but it isn't until he says her name that I realize he's arguing with Miss Hawthorne.

I have no idea what is going on.

"You know she's awake," Miss Hawthorne says. "I'm going to get us all some tea. You can explain the mess she's been dumped into while I'm doing that."

I hear the clicks of her high heels fading as she moves away from us. I sink farther down into the cushion I'm lying on as Jensen sits near my legs.

"Hey," he whispers, grabbing the top of my toes.

My heart starts racing.

"You don't have to pretend you're still unconscious, Genevieve."

I open my eyes. The expression on Jensen's face is unreadable, but his clenched jaw and taut lips suggest he's not in the best mood. I break away from his gaze and survey my surroundings. I'm lying on a white chaise longue in the middle of a huge, high-ceilinged room. There are several other pieces of expensive furniture meticulously arranged, as well as a large mahogany bookshelf covering the entirety of the wall across from me. To my side, the floor-to-ceiling windows look out onto a breathtaking landscape of flowers, shrubbery, and flowing creek. The crimson drapes are pulled back and tied by golden tassels, and the white-washed marble floor is illuminated even more so by the beams of light coming from the silver-encrusted chandeliers.

"We're in Sadie's home," Jensen says. "And you've been out for about an hour. Maybe a little more."

I look back at him, and the memory of the forest surges into my head. I can feel my breath quickening and my heart starting up in double-time. I retract my legs from him and pull them closer to my body.

He frowns. "You're afraid of me now." He sighs, shaking his head as he drops it to his chest. "Please don't be afraid of me, Genevieve."

I only look at him, not knowing what to say. His tensed posture melts away into a slumped defeat, and I can tell he's genuinely hurt. I reach out and touch his shoulder with my fingertips.

"I'm not afraid of you, Jensen." Which is a lie. "I'm just confused."

He lifts his head and nods. "Yes, I can imagine." He folds his arms and sighs, looking at me with his hypnotic, dark brown eyes. "May I try to explain what's going on?"

What am I supposed to say? *No, that's okay. Shooting fire from your hands is no big deal. To each his own.*

He moves closer to me, and I try not to look alarmed.

"Okay, so let's start with the obvious." Jensen inhales deeply. "I'm a mage." He releases his breath. "A fire mage, to be more exact."

"Okay."

"Okay?"

"Okay. You're a mage. A fire mage."

"Genevieve...I don't think you understand what I'm saying—"

"No, I get it." My voice is more high-pitched than usual. "My brother plays tons of video games, and I read all sorts of fantasy books, so I know exactly what a mage is. Shooting magic from your hands, conjuring spells, waving your magic wands. *Pew, pew.*"

"I think you're in shock—"

"No. I'm fine."

"Genevieve, please sit back down."

I don't remember standing up, but I'm aware now that I'm on my feet and halfway across the room, near the bookshelf. I move back over to the longue and lower myself onto its cushion, feeling exhaustion rush over my body.

"I'm sorry," I whisper, trying to control my shaky voice. "I'm sorry."

He places his hand on top of mine. His warmth

seeps deep into my skin.

"You have nothing to be sorry for," he whispers. "Your reaction is natural."

I take a deep breath. "So...you're a mage."

He nods slowly. "Sadie is, too. So is the boy you met in the woods."

"Scythe."

"Yeah." He grimaces. "Scythe."

Just keep cool, Genevieve. My mind begins working overtime. *Nothing's impossible.*

"And I doubt you're the only ones?" I say. "I mean, there are others?"

Again, Jensen nods.

"Is Scythe here, too?"

"No, he isn't with us. He's not on our side."

On our side. "So he's against you guys?"

"That's probably the best way to put it, yes."

"Against you for what?"

Jensen sighs. "It's complicated to explain. But I'll try," he says, when he sees the glare I'm throwing at him. "We're part of a magical group known as Formulists. Our history is complex and dates back a very long time. But certain individuals found that they had unique abilities. Some able to manifest fire. Or others, ice. There were even warriors whose skills were enhanced with different types of magic. Because these powers took on various forms, our namesake was established. It should come as no surprise that people who had these types of magical powers were considered dangerous by those who didn't. The Formulists became the target of much hatred and violence during the Crusades in the eleventh century, ultimately ending in the majority of Formulists being murdered or executed. In order to save ourselves, a new world had to be discovered, one where we could live freely and harness our powers. Several members of the Formulists diligently worked on establishing a realm for safety. And in their pursuit, they opened a portal to another world, a rift that linked the physical and the magical together. They called it Banewind."

"So people with magic existed on Earth before the discovery of your world?" I say.

Jensen shrugs. "We're not exactly sure how they came to be. Maybe people from Banewind crossed over to Earth in more ancient times. But all we know is that Formulists were present here, surviving for centuries before finding Banewind and making that our new home."

I let his words soak in.

"What are you thinking?" he says.

I shrug. "I'm just trying to convince myself that this is an actual conversation I'm having."

Jensen laughs. "That may take more time than you think."

"So you're a fire mage. And I'm guessing Scythe is an ice mage, then?"

I remember the snowy spells Scythe was casting in the forest. And the ice I slipped on while walking Grendel. It starts to make more sense.

"Right." Jensen nods. "Sadie is an ice mage, too." He pauses. "She's also my aunt."

"And why exactly are you here?" I say.

Miss Hawthorne's heels resonate through the mansion as she enters from an alcove at the opposite end of the room.

"I've got some delicious tea," she sings, placing the silver tray down on the table in front of the chaise longue. "Genevieve, hot or iced?"

"Iced."

I watch as she pours a cup full of steaming hot tea from a titanium kettle. Once full, she takes hold of the cup and the tea crackles and hisses as the porcelain frosts over.

"There." She hands me the cup on a matching saucer. "One of the advantages of being an ice mage." A look of horror washes over her face. "Oh! Wait a minute. You guys *did* talk about the mages, right?" She looks from me to Jensen.

"Jensen filled me in...and also just told me you're his aunt."

"Oh, excellent." She relaxes as she grabs her own cup of tea and settles into a nearby loveseat. "And call me Sadie, please."

I take a sip of tea. The cool liquid feels good running down my throat. I hadn't realized how thirsty I was.

"Thank you." I motion the cup to her.

She bats her hand as if shooing away a fly.

"No trouble at all." She blows on her own scalding hot tea and smooths out her dress. "So fill me in on what you two have been talking about."

"He was just telling me about the Formulists," I say. "You mentioned there are also warriors?"

"Yeah," Jensen says. "There are physical powers and elemental powers. Mages, as well as some of the other types of Formulists, are able to manipulate things like fire, ice, shadows, earth, or water. The warriors use weapons to enhance their powers, including holy magic or dark magic."

I think back to the numerous fantasy books I've read.

"Holy magic...like paladins?"

Jensen smiles. "Exactly."

"Warriors with dark magic are known as Void Knights," Sadie says. "As their power is said to come from

Banewind's ethereal void, or the Darkness. Before opening the portal to Banewind, dark magic didn't exist here on Earth. Legend has it that a fierce deity known as Ic'thyl was unleashed when the rift between worlds was created. And it was his corrupting power that brought forth the Darkness into existence."

"I'm trying to follow along." I feel my eyebrows furrow. "But I still don't understand why you guys are here if you have your own world."

Jensen and Sadie glance at each other.

"What?" I lean forward in my seat. "What is it?"

"This next part is hard to explain." Jensen sighs. "We, um...we came here to protect *you*, Genevieve."

"I'm sorry?"

"Your mother was a paladin, Genevieve," Sadie whispers. "So there is a chance that you are as well."

"No...that...you're joking, right?"

"It's true. She was a paladin. But when she gave birth to you, she decided to permanently sever her ties from the Formulists' world and concentrate on raising a family." Sadie's eyes are filled with sorrow. "As much as it pained us to do, we honored her wishes."

"You're lying," I choke out, and my face feels hot and flushed. "That's not possible."

Sadie stands and walks over to a desk near the bookshelf. She removes a picture from it and brings it back over to me.

"Here." She places the frame on my lap. "That's two years before she met your father. We were best friends."

I grab hold of the frame with shaking hands, and slowly bring it up to my face, allowing my vision to take in the faded picture. I recognize my mother, young and vivacious as she stands with her hip cocked next to Sadie, a huge smile spread across her face. Both women are wearing gorgeous white cloaks, and have their arms tossed over each other's shoulders.

I drop the picture onto the table, and my teacup tumbles over the side, crashing onto the marble floor and erupting into several pieces.

"I'm sorry," I mutter, feeling as though my body has gone numb.

Sadie takes a cloth from the tray and soaks up the spilt tea while picking up the pieces. She lays them out in her hand, and I watch in awe as a blue light swirls around the porcelain, mending the pieces back together with frosted ice filling in the cracks.

"There." She wads up the cloth and places it back onto the table. "Good as new." She sets down the teacup and returns to her seat. "You weren't supposed to discover any of this yet, Genevieve. We were going to tell you eventually, but not like this."

"But you...you think that...you think that *I'm* a paladin?"

"Addisyn was not only a paladin," Sadie says, "but she was what we call the Holy Guardian—a lineage of female paladins who fought against the Darkness and protected the royal Banewind family. The same family the land was named after. As such, it is possible that you are also a paladin, and maybe even the next Holy Guardian, as you are Addisyn's only daughter."

I pull apart each of her words, trying to dissect exactly what it is I'm hearing. My mother, the kind, compassionate woman who would sing me to sleep at night when I was a child. The woman who sat me on her lap as she read to me countless hours, introducing me to the magical worlds that existed between the pages of *The Wind in the Willows* or *The Lion, the Witch, and the Wardrobe.* The woman who bought me my first journal, who taught me that crying was not a weakness, but a sign of strong emotion. The woman who kissed my bruises and scared the monsters away from under my bed.

My mother, who had an entire life I knew nothing about.

"I don't know what to say," I whisper, my voice cracking.

I glance again at the picture lying on the table.

"I just...I can't believe it."

"Regardless of whether you believe it or not, you're in danger," Jensen says. "There is a group of Formulists known as the Voidweavers, who have attempted to destroy Banewind for many years now. They worship Ic'thyl, and their only goal is to see the Darkness rise to power. Your mother protected us from them. But unfortunately, they have returned."

"Scythe is working with the Voidweavers, trying to capture you." Sadie says. "Your mother destroyed their leader, the Void King, ten years ago. She gave her life to do so, but she saved our world. And yours as well."

"But the Voidweavers believe that since you are her descendent," Jensen says, "you could be a key to bringing him back. One of our allies, Mengurion Maldridge—a well-respected fire mage who has lived through decades of this war—warned us of their ploy. Unfortunately, he was captured by the Voidweavers weeks ago, and we haven't heard from him since."

"But we know that what Maldridge says is true," Sadie says. "He is one of the wisest men I know. A father figure to many. He was a mentor to your mother and I. And he knows better than anyone the events that plague

Banewind." She pauses. "It was his warning that set us out to look for you. And so here we are."

"So my mother...didn't die in a car accident? She was killed by...the Void King?"

Their silence is enough of an answer for me.

"Your mother loved you so much, Genevieve," Sadie says. "Her family was her top priority, her life's joy." Her eyes are glistening. "She walked away from Banewind in hopes to live out the rest of her days with you and your family. But when the Void King threatened the existence of life itself, she took up her mantle to return to Banewind and defeat him in order to save you...to save everyone."

"And she did." Jensen reaches over and squeezes my hand. "She was a hero."

"And you're positive they're after me?" The goosebumps spread across my skin. "But why? I don't have any powers."

"Not that you know of," Sadie says. "But that doesn't mean you won't. You haven't been raised as a paladin."

"I think I'm going to be sick." I feel queasy, hot, and sweaty. "This is too much."

"I agree." Jensen looks at Sadie. "She's heard enough today. I'm going to take her back home." He smiles at me. "We'll talk more about it soon. I promise."

I nod mechanically as I stand from the couch. Jensen and Sadie walk behind me as we head to the front door.

"Does my father know about this?" I say, not sure if I'm ready to hear the answer.

"People keep secrets from each other, Genevieve," says Sadie. "Sometimes it's for the best."

This isn't an answer to my question, but I'm too exhausted to discuss it anymore.

"I'll see you tomorrow," Sadie says, as we step outside. "Try to get some sleep."

We sit in silence the entire ride home. I keep myself focused by looking out the window, watching as one after another, the streetlamps whiz by. My mind is numb, and I have so many thoughts rushing through my head from what I just learned that I don't even have time to comprehend them.

When we finally pull into my driveway, I unbuckle my seatbelt, but sit frozen in Jensen's red Jeep, unable to move any further.

"Genevieve," he whispers. "Are you okay?"

"I don't know. I just...I don't know."

"That's understandable." His voice is calm and comforting. "Do you need anything from me right now?"

I shake my head. "I just need some time to digest this." I open the door and hesitate before I step out. "Am I... am I safe?" The words choke in my throat. "I mean...well, am I?"

"Sadie and I will be keeping an eye on you. I promise. We won't let anything happen."

I step onto the driveway, my legs heavy like lead pipes.

"What do I do now?"

"Nothing. We can talk more about this in the morning. You can call me if you need anything."

I nod, trying to hold back tears.

"Thank you," I whisper. "I'll see you tomorrow."

I start walking up the driveway.

"Hey, Genevieve." He sticks his head out the driver's window. "It's going to be okay."

I watch as his Jeep disappears down the street.

As I pass my car, I'm horrified to see my reflection in the mirror. I'm covered in soot from when I was in the forest.

I take off my pink sweater and stuff it in the bottom of the trash can so no one will see it. I walk around to the side of the house and turn on the hose, then dip my hands into the cold water and rub it over my arms until almost all of the grime has been removed. Once I feel presentable, I head through the side door.

"Nice of you to join us."

I hear my dad's voice from the family room, and turn and see him sitting with his laptop and several papers scattered around the coffee table. He doesn't look happy.

Crap.

"Hi, Dad." I try to sound energetic. "Sorry I'm home so late. I got tied up at a friend's house, and I didn't realize what time—"

"Don't give me excuses, Jeannie. Do you know how irresponsible this was of you? Your brother has been home by himself for most of the evening, and he nearly burnt down the house trying to cook dinner." He gestures to the sink, and I see a burnt frying pan as black as night, submerged in soapy water. "On top of that, there was apparently a fire in the forest earlier today. The fire trucks were just leaving the street as I got home. What if something had happened to him while he was by himself?"

"I'm sorry," I murmur, kicking my foot on the floor.

My dad takes off his glasses and sets them next to his laptop.

"It's okay." He sighs as his voice melts away into softness. "I shouldn't be so hard on you. Truthfully, I don't give you enough credit for everything you do around here for us." A grin broadens across his face. "So one mess up isn't going to hurt you too badly."

"Thanks, Dad. I'm going to go shower and read a little."

I have to get out of here before he notices my appearance and starts asking questions.

"Wait a minute, Jeannie. The neighbors called for you."

Oh, crap. No! The dog. I forgot all about him, and I never got him back from the woods.

"Shoot! I'll run over there right now. I'm sorry, Dad. I totally—"

"Whoa, whoa, honey." He raises his brow. "You don't have to go over there. Everything's fine. They just wanted to thank you and your friend for taking care of Grendel today." He chuckles. "And I'll admit, even I was surprised to hear you'd do that for Daniel. I'm sure he promised you something in exchange, right?"

"Yeah, he's going to wash my car. I don't understand. What do you mean they wanted to thank me and *my friend*?"

He shrugs. "I don't know all your friends, Jeannie. They just said to thank you and the boy in the blue tracksuit." He smiles. "Is this a new boy...?"

"What? Oh, no. Katie and Floyd were with me."

The boy in the blue tracksuit...

Scythe.

"Oh, okay."

He puts on his glasses and goes back to reading his papers.

"There are leftovers in the refrigerator if you want them. I'm going to be hitting the hay soon myself."

"Thanks," I finally head into the foyer. "Night, Dad."

As I head up the stairs, I still can't shake the idea of

Scythe returning the dog for me. I mean, he *is* trying to kill me, after all...right?

I can't think straight anymore. I just need a long, hot shower. And my bed. But even after I wash off and climb under the covers, sleep evades me.

People keep secrets from each other. Sadie's words jump into my head. *Sometimes it's for the best.*

I get out of bed and put on my purple slippers, then slowly open the bedroom door. The hallway is dark, and the only noise I hear is the muffled snores of my father, coming from his room. I creep down the stairs, tiptoe to the basement door, and gingerly shut it behind me.

The storage room is filled to the brim with all sorts of knick-knacks collected through the years. The Christmas tree leans against the unfinished wall, where several boxes of ornaments are stacked precariously on top of one another. Bins of schoolwork from my elementary years are tucked away next to a broken treadmill, untouched since they were originally placed. I find the area where we keep our old family photos, too many containers to even count.

"Where is it?" I pull open different lids to find what I'm looking for. "Come on. I know you're here somewhere."

As I move one of the containers, I finally see what I'm searching for sitting behind it, labeled, *Mom's Stuff.*

I take a deep breath and pull it from the shelf, then remove the lid. The stale plastic smell tickles my nostrils, and I sneeze. I sit on the floor and rummage through the items inside. There are several scrapbooks, half-completed, with various images of myself as a child.

"Oh, God." I laugh, remembering the phase my mother went through when she was trying to catalogue every moment of our lives.

I see a picture of myself at Halloween, when I

was no more than three or four years old, dressed up like Sherlock Holmes. I flip the page, and there I am in between my mother and father, holding a bright yellow Easter egg out for the camera.

I close the book and set it aside. As I dig through the box more, I find an unlabeled manila envelope. I open it, and my mother's memorial card from the funeral home falls into my lap. Her face stares up at me, smiling. Like she had never really left.

I reach into the envelope and pull out a handful of pictures, all taken at her funeral.

Weird. Who takes photos at a funeral?

But that day is a distant memory, and even now I can still only remember bits and pieces of what happened.

"I'm so sorry for your loss," someone would say.

"How tragic. Victor DeWinter left alone to raise the children."

"She was so young. It isn't fair."

I flip through the photos and stop to look at pictures from the cemetery—me holding my dad's hand next to the mausoleum. Katie and her family. Me sitting on the couch at the funeral home, with a plate of food resting on my lap, and a boy next to me.

Wait. What?

I pull the photo closer, studying the boy in the picture. He's smiling at the camera, with his head resting on my shoulder, eating a pastry. His brown eyes are so familiar. He might be ten years younger, but even so, I can recognize Jensen Saint Clair.

I scan the rest of the photos, my heart racing as I peruse the various images. More flowers, more people, more memorials.

I pull the photo I'm holding closer to me, and freeze.

"No way."

My father is standing outside the hearse as several men, including Katie's father, are lined up at my mother's casket. But that isn't what catches my attention.

To my dad's left is a woman in a black dress, her hand resting against my father's back, her profile visible as she stares out into the distance, a forlorn expression washed across her face.

There is no mistaking her.

No mistaking Sadie Hawthorne as she consoles my weeping father.

7

FOR LEASE

NEEDLESS TO SAY, THE REST OF MY NIGHT IS UNEASY. I have so many different scenarios running through my head that the only thing I'm doing is creating a constant loop of anxiety.

That Sadie and Jensen were at my mother's funeral suggests that my father at least knew about them. But to what extent? Was he aware of who they really were and where they came from? Clearly, he looks close to Sadie in that photo.

But beyond that?

So many possibilities.

So many lies. So many secrets.

I decide to try and get more info from Jensen and Sadie before confronting him about it. I arrive at school and head into homeroom, where Jensen and Katie are already seated.

"Morning!" Katie says, as I sit next to her. "How are you?"

"Tired. I didn't sleep very well last night." I look at Jensen. "I had a lot on my mind."

"Everything okay?" Jensen has his arms crossed

against his chest.

"Well—"

"Okay, class, settle down." Sadie stands from her desk.

I'm grateful I don't have to answer Jensen at the moment.

"Today we're going to do our first lab on the microscope." She starts passing around papers. "I've already assigned you lab partners to work with this semester. You can look on the attached sheet."

"Thanks." I grab the papers.

She smiles at me before moving to the next row.

I scan the document for my lab partner. *Genevieve DeWinter and Jensen Saint Clair.*

"Oh, lucky," Katie whispers. "Look who you're with."

"Yeah, I see that." I throw a look to Jensen. "That's convenient."

After Sadie runs through the objectives with us, we head to the back of the room to the lab benches. I grab my binder, notebook, and the manila envelope with the photos in it.

"What's wrong?" Jensen pulls the cover off the microscope. "Did something happen?"

"You mean, something more than everything you already told me yesterday?" I grab the box of slides from the drawer. "Amazingly, yes." I pull the photos from the envelope and place them in front of him. "We need to focus the microscope first," I say, loudly, as another student passes by, then slide the photos to Jensen and whisper, "Look at what I found last night."

I watch as he flips through the photos, confusion emerging onto his face.

"What are these?"

"Switch the lens to the ten-times objective." I play with the knobs on the microscope as I look around to make sure no one is listening to our conversation. "Photos from my mother's funeral. Do you recognize anyone?"

"I don't...I don't remember this." He stares at the picture of himself. "I was there?"

"Apparently so." I place a slide into the holder. "I mean, we were eight, Jensen. I'm not surprised you can't recall some random funeral from a decade ago."

"That's my father." He points to one of the men carrying my mother's casket. "So your dad knew about us?"

"I don't know, Jensen!"

The students at the lab bench across the aisle look over at us.

"Um, I don't know! Try the forty-times power."

"Everything going all right, you two?" Sadie approaches the lab bench. "Have any questions?"

Jensen hands her the photos.

Her face pales. "Where did you get these?" She stares at the photo of herself.

"They were in our basement," I say. "I was looking through my mother's stuff last night when I got home, seeing if I could find anything more. So my dad *did* know about my mother?"

"Miss Hawthorne, where are the planaria?" A student says, from across the room.

"Over in the lab hood." She motions to the back corner. "The cutting tools are there as well." She looks back at the photos before setting them down. "Your father knew about the Formulists, yes." She holds up a finger. "But only of their existence and your mother's powers. He never visited Banewind. He never interacted with anyone else, and your mother never told him anymore than he needed to know."

"Well, he interacted with you! And Jensen's family."

"Yes, he knew about us because we were your mother's best friends. She never wanted him to know about Banewind or the Formulists. But when we had to bring her back to face the Void King, he found out about us. There was no way your mother could keep it from him anymore. Especially when she knew she might not return to you."

"And we went to her funeral?" Jensen says.

Sadie nods. "After that, we left and never returned."

"So my father knew my mother wasn't killed in a car accident?" I shake my head. "He knows how she really died?"

"He didn't tell you for good reason, Genevieve," Sadie says.

I'm sure she can see the anger in my eyes.

"You were eight, and Danny was three. You weren't old enough to even understand what was going on."

"I can't believe this." I gasp.

"How's it going, guys?" Katie approaches us, a smile spread across her face.

We stare at her like deer in headlights.

"Oh...uh, everything okay?" she says.

"Fine." I place another slide onto the microscope. "Just peachy."

"Okay...I'll...let you get back to work."

"Any issues, Miss Miller?" Sadie says, a false-hearted smile on her face. "Do you need my assistance?"

"No, we're good." She turns to head back to her lab bench. "Just saying hello."

I know she's still staring at me, but I don't look back. I'm not sure I'd be able to keep from breaking down. And keeping this from Katie right now is hard enough as it is. She's my best friend. We confide in each other with everything. This isn't fair.

"Genevieve," Sadie says. "I understand that all of this is a lot. I do. But you cannot blame your father. Or your mother, for that matter. Please."

I let out an exasperated sigh. "I know."

"Did you mention this to your father yet?" she says.

"No." I shake my head. "I don't...I don't know what good that would do right now. It's all too much."

"Miss Hawthorne?" Another student raises her hand.

"We'll talk more later." Sadie looks at the microscope. "Make sure you're documenting the correct magnification, please." She walks away.

"I'm sorry," Jensen says. "I wish I were more helpful, too. There's obviously a lot I don't know about."

"It's fine." I put my eyes to the microscope lenses. "Let's just get through this class."

When lunch period rolls around, I find Jensen already in the cafeteria.

"Hey." I sit next to him. "I want to know more about these Voidweavers."

"Is this really the place?" He looks around the cafeteria. "Your friends are going to come eat with us, aren't they?"

"Katie's doing something with band recital, and Floyd's with the robotics team again. Now's the perfect time."

"I see." Jensen stares at his half-eaten cheeseburger. "You know, your food here really isn't that good. I thought it would be a lot better."

"No school's food is edible, Jensen. Don't avoid my question."

"I'm not." He laughs. "I was just making a statement."

"The Voidweavers. Tell me."

He sighs. "Banewind was ruled by several different families up until the last decade. One of the families ruled the sky. Another, the seas. And the last, the Banewind family, ruled the land of Banewind itself. Your mother, and the rest of the Holy Guardians, protected our society from any threat or destruction. They were thought to be descendants of the goddess Lura, the creator of holy magic. The Voidweavers were a group of zealots against everything that the ruling families stood for, with most of their hatred directed towards the Holy Guardians. Their leader was a man named Ganstin Remores, and it was he who became known as the Void King. He was a powerful, malevolent man. And with his insatiable thirst for destruction, the Voidweavers grew strong enough to destroy most of the land. Once they overpowered everyone and everything, they turned their sights onto the final thing holding it all together—the Banewind family. A war ensued against the Voidweavers, and it was your mother who dealt the final blow to the Void King. Both she and her mentor, Dorndrick Wolfshire, one of the best male paladins known to Banewind, led their army to victory. But by the time that battle happened, the Void King had already killed all the Banewind family. Once it was over, the people decided to end the monarchial system, letting it die out with the family's memory. The Council of the Formulists, which consists of representatives from different regions of the land, was decided to be given rule, and thus the current democracy of Banewind was born."

"But you said the Voidweavers are looking for me because they're trying to revive the Void King. How is that possible if he's dead?"

"You remember Sadie mentioning Mengurion Maldridge? The elderly mage who the Voidweavers captured?"

"Yeah."

"He's informed us that a woman known as the Dark Lady is leading them now. When your mother killed the Void King, she sealed him away. The Voidweavers believe that if they can find the same power used by your mother, they could return him to his former self. Since the time of the final battle, they have hunted down paladins and past Holy Guardians, trying to find someone who may have had your mother's blood. They've killed almost all of them now—in vain, of course, because none of them had direct ties to her. And without that, the Void King remains imprisoned. We pleaded with the Council of the Formulists to do something to help us. My father is one of the members. But they were stubborn, unwilling to do so because you aren't from Banewind. They said their resources could go to better use in the fight against the Voidweavers. My family and I shared our thoughts with Sadie and decided that she and I would have to be the ones to come here and protect you ourselves."

"So this can all be put to an end if the Void King is destroyed for good?" I grab Jensen's arm. "Then why don't we do that? Let's stop him."

He shakes his head. "It isn't that easy. We don't know *how* to do that. Your mother locked him away, yes. But we don't know anything more than that. We don't even know how to find him, let alone what we would do to end him for good."

"If I am a paladin," I feel my heart quicken, "then

maybe *I* can destroy him."

"What? Genevieve, no—"

"You all said yourself that I would be the next Holy Guardian. It makes sense, Jensen."

"In theory, sure. But that's putting a lot at stake."

"This entire situation is putting a lot at stake. If I can help prevent the Voidweavers' success, then I want to do just that." I feel my confidence growing. "I want to be like my mother."

The warning bell for class rings.

"What do you think?" I stare at Jensen and can tell he's deep in thought.

"It's possible." He looks at me and frowns. "But also very dangerous."

"Well, we can discuss it more with Sadie this weekend. How about that?" I start packing up my bags. "Deal?"

He groans. "You're very persistent." A smile spreads across his face. "But deal."

I've grown excited at the prospect that I could follow in my mother's footsteps.

All my life, I have read fantasy books about good and evil, light and dark, right and wrong. From the first moments I could read, my mother had made sure I had a book in my hands, encouraging me to seek further knowledge in the fantastical. I reflect back and wonder now if she had been trying to prepare me for this, knowing that even with her hope she could separate herself from the magical world she was from, the chance that it could spill over into my life was always a possibility. Knowing that one day, I could face the same tribulations she was up against.

There's so much I don't yet understand. Who knows

what even lies ahead.

The rest of the day passes by, and after finishing my homework I go to bed early, the exhaustion finally catching up to me. I'm able to avoid my dad, as he is busy working at the university, still not sure if I want to broach the subject of my mother with him yet. That can be a task for another day.

The next morning, Katie picks me up for school.

"Hey," she says, when I get into her car. "I didn't hear much from you yesterday. Is everything okay?"

"Hey, yeah, it's fine."

Guilt washes over me as I continue to keep my best friend out of the important updates of my life. I can tell she knows something is up.

"You excited for our dates tonight?" I say.

Her face brightens. "Yes! I can't wait." She giggles. "I haven't been to the movies all summer. Floyd texted me and said he'd like to see the new *Macbeth*. You okay with that?"

"Absolutely." I smile. "That's in the top three of my favorite Shakespeare plays."

"Oh, I know." She grins. "Remember when we made that ridiculous movie freshman year? We re-adapted the entire thing, using only rhyming couplets."

"Hey, I was very proud of that script I wrote." I laugh. "It's done! It's done! Duncan is dead!"

"Calm down, fool. Get ahold of your head!" Katie recites back, mimicking Lady Macbeth.

Our laughter fills the car as we approach the school.

I hear the car horn honk just as I finish curling my hair.

"Have fun on your date, Vee," Danny says, as I throw on my cream cardigan.

My dad looks up from his work at the kitchen table and stares at me over the top of his glasses.

"You have a date tonight?" The surprise in his voice is obvious. "Who is he?"

"Just some new guy from school."

I tease my hair one more time while I'm next to the mirror in the foyer. I'm still trying to avoid any prolonged conversations with him.

"We're showing him around. You know, trying to make him feel welcome."

"Yeah, in a dark movie theater." Danny giggles. "Try not to get mono."

"Do you even know what mono is?" My father laughs as he stands from his chair, and comes over to pull me to his chest.

"Dad! My hair." I try to resist his hug.

Only after I return the embrace does he let his arms drop.

"You be safe tonight, Jeannie." He gives my forehead a peck. "And don't get pressured into doing anything you aren't comfortable with. Remember, it's okay to say no."

"Dad..." I feel my face flush red with embarrassment. "It isn't like that. Trust me."

"Well, if things do go that way, remember to use protection, okay?"

"Oh, my God!" I cover my ears. "This conversation isn't happening. Goodbye."

I slam the front door shut, but can still hear Danny cracking up.

"He's so immature." I scoff.

The horn honks again.

"I'm coming!" I run down the driveway and can see Katie waving at me through the windshield.

"You look hot." She chuckles as I settle into passenger seat. "You're really trying to impress him, huh?"

"Oh, stop it." I bite my lip, attempting to hide my smile. "I mean, it's not that obvious, is it?"

Katie laughs. "Aww. It's so cute that you have a crush."

"Well, what about you?" I point to the hoop earrings she wears. "I don't even remember the last time I've seen you with jewelry."

"Is it too much?" Her words are coated with worry as she looks into the rearview mirror. "Should I take them out?"

"No, you look beautiful. Trust me. Floyd won't know what hit him."

"Remind me again why we come to this place?" Katie groans as we walk into the mall.

Droves of people are flooding the entryway.

"Because it's the only decent movie theater we have around here," I reply. "Unless you want to drive thirty minutes into Westlake."

Katies grimaces. "Ugh, I'm sure it's ten times worse there." She looks at her watch. "We're a little early. You want to look around at some stores? I was hoping to find a cute dress to wear to Homecoming." She glances over the posed mannequins in the display windows. "I'm hoping Floyd will want to go with me."

"Of course he will. You've gone with him, what, the last two years?" I giggle. "You really should just be dating already."

"Genevieve, look!" She gasps as she grabs a hold of my arm. "It's gorgeous."

"It looks expensive." I'm eyeing the Versace navy blue dress.

"Oh, I have to try it on." She runs to the store's entrance. "You coming?"

"Why don't I go wait by the theater in case anyone shows up?" I wave her into the store. "You go on ahead. I'll tell Floyd you're getting something pretty for him."

"Cut it out." She laughs. "Text me when the boys show up."

I find the escalator and take it down to the lower level, where the movie theater is located. The food court is nearby, and there are several novelty stores scattered around the perimeter, but it's less crowded than the rest of the mall. Since there is almost no line outside the box office yet, I decide to look around while I countdown the minutes until I see Jensen.

As I'm browsing through the various selections of sunglasses at a nearby kiosk, I notice there's a new store I'm not familiar with. The display windows are tinted red and fogged over so I can't see into them, and there's no sign to identify what the shop even is. A maroon sheet hangs over the door alcove, with little light creeping out from beneath it.

I grab the sheet and pull it to the side, poking my head into the alcove to see if anyone is there. For some reason, my heart's beating faster, and I feel like I'm doing something wrong.

"Hello?" I look around the shop.

The wallpaper is a deep purple, and there are several hanging lights draped with red veils, causing an eerie glow to illuminate the room. There are jewels and wind chimes dangling from the ceiling, and their melodic clinking creates a soothing ambience, which fades into haunting echoes. In the middle of the room is a small table with a lit candelabrum, and behind it sits a figure with a black veil concealing its face.

"Oh!" I say.

The figure doesn't move.

"I'm sorry. I didn't mean to bother you." I draw back the sheet.

"Nonsense, child. You aren't disturbing me."

Sounds like a woman's voice.

"Please, come in."

I hesitate. This seems like a bad idea.

"I'll stop by another time." I back out of the doorway. "Thank you, though."

"There won't be another time, Genevieve."

My shoulders tense. "You know who I am?" I try not to show my fright. "Are you..."

"A Formulist? More or less." She chuckles.

Jensen should really be here with you.

"Don't worry. You're safe without Mister Saint Clair. Oh, don't look so surprised." She motions to the chair across from her. "Now please, have a seat."

Part of me wants to run. There's no way to tell if this woman can be trusted, and it would be better to just get out of there. Yet I have a feeling she's on my side. I can't explain why, but my intuition is directing me to talk with her. So I approach the chair and sit.

"Excellent," the woman says, as I scoot the chair towards the table. "You had the courage to come in and sit down with me—a crucial step which forms the cornerstone of our relationship." She folds her hands in front of her.

"Next, we must build up trust."

"Who are you?" I whisper.

"My name is Ilona." Her voice sounds distant and carries an echo, as if it traveled miles through a cave to reach my ears. "And you, my dear, are Genevieve DeWinter."

She pulls the long sleeves back on her maroon robe. The black gloves she wears travel to her elbows.

"It is an honor to meet you," she says.

"I'm not sure about that."

Ilona's laugh reverberates around the room.

"In time, you'll see. But you must be patient."

"What do you want with me?" I start to feel nervous again.

"I want to guide you, Genevieve. Your future is not an easy one."

I can't tell, but I think she's looking at me.

"Genevieve, a war will soon dawn upon the horizon, and you are going to be an essential key to its inevitable arrival."

My heart is racing. "A war? Between who?"

"Everyone."

I wait for her to say more, but she sits in silence.

"Why, then?"

She shakes her head. "You are not ready for that answer."

I huff in frustration. "Well, what question should I ask? What's the point of you trying to help me if you aren't going to reveal anything?"

"I am not here to reveal. I told you, I am merely here to guide you."

"Right." I lean back in the chair and fold my arms. "Okay, so then what can you help me with?"

Ilona stands from her chair and glides to the back

of the store. On a shelf sits a small porcelain bowl and a purple pitcher that she picks up and brings to the table. She sets them next to the candelabrum as she returns to her seat.

"I have something for you." She picks up the pitcher and pours its contents into the bowl.

Once it is full, she pushes it towards me. My face is reflected in the silver liquid's pool.

"I want you to imagine your mother." She waves her hand over the bowl. "Think of the memories you have with her. Picture her face. Feel her presence."

At the mention of my mother, I feel the familiarity of a large lump forming in my throat. Even after all this time, any memory stirred unravels a myriad of emotions.

I stare into the bowl and watch as my mother emerges below the surface. She's standing there, wearing the same white cloak from the picture I saw her in at Sadie's house. The image is replaced by her kneeling on a picnic blanket, with me by her side. She holds a bubble wand with one hand, tears in her eyes from laughing as I see my toddler self, clapping at the air as I try to snatch the floating spheres. They disappear with a small *pop!* and I gasp, then let out a high-pitched giggle. She picks me up and swings me around in the air.

"*Genevieve.*" I hear her voice in my head. Soothing and calm, gentle and warm. "*Genevieve, my sweet girl.*"

The scene morphs as suddenly as it appeared. I see my mother's face, bruised and beaten. Her blonde hair is stuck to her forehead, caked with blood. She staggers across a black marble floor, the ground jagged and cracked. She's draped in silver armor, with shoulder pauldrons shaped like owls with sapphires set in their eye sockets. She extends her hands, wrapped around a dazzling metal hammer radiating with golden hues and bright light as if she had taken the weapon from the Norse god Thor himself.

"I will not let you win," I hear my mother's words, her voice raspy and broken. *"The Void King will not succeed, and his memory will fade into nothing...even if I have to give my life to make sure it is so."*

Black shadows cloud the memory until bright amethyst eyes stare back at me, obscured by the darkness. They are terrifying and piercing, like shattered glass cutting through flesh.

"See me," a booming, male voice echoes through my skull. *"See me and know I am always watching. I have always been watching. And I will always be watching."*

A shriek fractures my ears, and the image burns into my mind. My heart pounds and my breathing grows shallow as an impending sense of dread fills my core. The outline of a towering male warrior emerges. His purple eyes still glow fervently through the shadows. A black cape flows down his back, with pauldrons shaped like giant skulls resting on each shoulder.

"See me now. See me, Genevieve!"

"What's happening!" I scream, but can't hear my own words.

A myriad of images explode across my vision as I watch in horror as wolf-like creatures snarl and snap, their mouths foaming. They morph into a dragon spewing black rays from its mouth, casting them over a vast lighthouse with a purple beacon projecting through the air. And then I'm screaming, falling into a darkened abyss. When I hit the ground, I see a blackened hand flail to grab me. As I cry out, the image evaporates and is replaced by a large bird skull and those same amethyst eyes burning behind the eye sockets.

And then there is stillness, and all goes quiet.

The image fades from my mind, and I am again staring at the bowl on the table in front of me. The silver liquid swirls into a small vortex, splashing against the porcelain like rough waves. When it settles, there is a coin-like object resting at the bottom.

"What...what just happened." I sit there, attempting to catch my breath.

Ilona sits behind the table, her calm demeanor jarring after the experience I just endured.

"Memories," she whispers. "Past, present, future. The scrying bowl shows you what it wants you to see." She motions to the object in the bowl. "Go ahead. Pick it up. It's all right."

I waver before touching my fingertips to the water. The cool liquid caresses my skin, and I can feel something more to it, like a surge of electricity. I grab the object from the bowl and hold it up in front of my face, straining to see it in the dim light.

"What is it?" I turn the object in my fingers.

One side of it is coated in silver, with the image of an eye on it. The eyelashes look like long, slender icicles, and the eyebrow above it resembles a rising flame. Along the perimeter of the coin are eight small circles, and the backside of it is black.

"It is the Formulists' insignia," Ilona says. "The eye represents the school of psychic magic. The flaming brow for fire, and the eyelashes signify ice."

"What are the circles for?"

"Shadow mages. The silver side symbolizes the holy magic of Lura, whereas the black backing represents the dark magic of Ic'thyl. Essentially, it is the core of the

Formulists' existence. The Blazing Vision."

"Why are you giving it to me?" I run my finger over the raised etching.

"To remind you of your destiny. This talisman once belonged to your mother. And now it shall belong to you."

"Genevieve!"

I hear my name shouted from outside the store, and flinch in my chair as I realize it is Jensen's voice.

"I'm afraid that's all the time we have together. For now, anyway." Ilona waves her hand over the bowl, and the silver light dies away, returning the liquid to a dark abyss. "You must go now. Mister Saint Clair is waiting for you."

I stand from the chair, keeping my gaze on Ilona as I rise.

"What do you want from me?"

Ilona laughs. "In time, you will see." She extends her hand towards the exit.

I slip the talisman into my jean pocket and head for the door.

"Genevieve?" she calls, as I'm about to step through the alcove.

I turn around to face her once more.

"Be safe."

I nod. "Thank you," I whisper.

I step out the door and back inside the bustling mall.

"There you are." Jensen darts over to me with a smile spread wide across his face, but his eyes are filled with concern. "Katie said you left to wait by the theater quite a bit ago." He frowns. "I was getting worried about you."

"Sorry. I got distracted doing something."

"Oh?" Jensen raises his eyebrows. "And what might that have been?"

"I went into that store over there and—" I turn to

point at Ilona's shop.

What had just been decorated with fogged windows, red sheets, and tinted lights, now lay barren. Propped up on the window's ledge is a large sign with bold letters that reads, FOR LEASE. PLEASE CALL FOR INQUIRIES.

"I don't understand." I approach the window to peer inside.

There is nothing but a dark, vacant room.

"Where did she go?"

I hear Jensen approach behind me. "We're going to be late for the movie."

I turn towards him, and he flashes a pair of tickets.

"Katie and Floyd are already at their seats."

"Yeah, okay." I glance back at the empty shop one last time. "Let's go."

As I walk next to Jensen, I realize I'm still trembling, shaken by what I've just experienced. I build up enough confidence to slip my hand into his, attempting to feel more secure. His fingers lock with mine, and fireworks explode inside my body.

"I hope this is a good movie," Jensen says, as we're about to enter the theater. "I've never really been a fan of Shakespeare. There's too much doom and gloom."

"You know Shakespeare?"

I'm surprised he'd be familiar with something outside of Banewind.

He laughs. "Hey, just because I'm from another world doesn't mean they don't educate us properly." He smiles. "I studied at our academy, which is one of the most prestigious institutes children can learn from in Banewind. Spent ten years of my life there."

"And they teach you Shakespeare?" I grin. "Even in another world, he's a cornerstone to literature, huh?"

Jensen laughs again. "He's up there, that's for sure."

He hands the tickets to the usher, who rips them in half and gives us each a piece. As I stuff the stub into my jean pocket, I feel a cold metal object touch the back of my hand.

The Blazing Vision. I recall the words Ilona spoke as I grasp the talisman. *See, Genevieve? You aren't crazy.*

The two of us enter the dark theater.

8

MACBETH

THE LIGHTS HAVE ALREADY DIMMED, and it takes a moment for my eyes to adjust to the darkness. The theater is jam-packed, and I can hear the whispers as people anxiously wait for the movie to begin.

I scan the rows for my friends, but don't see any familiar faces.

"Do you know where they're sitting?" I turn to Jensen.

"I think they're down at the front."

He grabs my hand, and my heart starts fluttering at his touch.

We head down the aisle and stop a couple rows from the very front. Katie is sitting in the aisle seat, and Floyd is next to her. But the rest of the row is full.

"Um, Katie?" I bend down next to her and whisper, "Where are our seats?"

Katie looks at me and bites her lip. "We tried to save them for you, but the theater was getting so full and people were really intimidating, so we couldn't hold onto them anymore." She drops her gaze to the floor. "I'm sorry, Jeannie."

I sigh. "It's okay. We'll find somewhere else to sit, and just meet you after the movie." I turn to Jensen. "Is that okay with you?"

"It doesn't bother me," he whispers back. "I think I saw some seats in the back."

"Ugh. Again, I'm so sorry." Katie pouts dramatically.

I can't help but laugh.

"Don't worry about it." I drop down right below her ear so only she can hear what I say. "Have fun with Floyd."

"Gen-e-*vieve!*"

Even in the theater's dimness, I can see her blushing.

Jensen leads us back up the aisle, where there are two seats on the end of a row. He lets me go in first, and I sit in the red velveteen cushion. The lights turn off, and the previews begin to play. Although there are several promising trailers, I'm too distracted by Jensen to concentrate on anything. He holds my hand in his lap, and I close my eyes, breathing him in, still awe-stricken by his overwhelming beauty.

I lay my head on his shoulder.

"Are you comfortable?" he whispers into my ear.

I can smell his breath, sweet and fresh.

"Mhm." I nod against him, and feel his lips press against my ear.

"Good. I'm glad." He takes my hand from his lap and pulls it up to his chest, clutching it against his body.

If I died right now, I wouldn't have a problem with that.

The movie starts playing, and I'm still having a hard time paying attention to the screen. I want so badly to just focus all my attention on Jensen. To watch him and stare into his eyes for hours and hours. I want to be able to hear his heartbeat and feel his body pressed against mine, warming me with his heat, his soul. My stomach is tying into knots, pulling at my heartstrings and causing my mind to race.

I don't want this to end.

I hold the same position on his shoulder for as long as I can without moving. But by the time Lady Macbeth has coerced her husband into killing Duncan, my neck is stiff, and I know if I don't move it soon, I'll risk ending up in this contorted position permanently.

"Are you okay?" He lets go of my hand so I can stretch in my seat.

I wince as I try to bring my head back into an upright position.

"Yeah, just stiff." *What a great way to kill the moment. You're acting like a ninety-year old grandma.* "Would, um... would you mind rubbing my neck?"

He looks at me and smiles. "Not at all."

He massages my skin, and I melt into his grasp. My muscles loosen, and every touch from him sends an electrifying jolt through my body, awakening all my senses.

"Does that feel better?"

"Oh, yes," I whisper back, and close my eyes. "Thank you."

"Psst. Genevieve."

I open my eyes and see Katie standing in the aisle next to Jensen.

"Katie?"

Jensen takes his hand off my neck.

"Oops, sorry," she whispers. "Am I interrupting?"

"Uh...no, it's okay. What's up?"

"Come to the bathroom with me."

"Oh, boy." I look at Jensen. "I'll be right back." I follow Katie out of the theater and into the restroom.

"What's going on? Are you okay?"

She turns and looks at me, beaming. "Floyd just kissed me!" Her braids bounce as she hops on her feet. "Oh, my gosh. Oh my gosh!"

I laugh. "What! During the movie?"

"Mhm. We were just sitting there holding hands, and then he turned to me and said, *I really like your glasses.* So then I turned to him and said, *I really like your glasses, too.* And then the next thing I know, his lips were on my lips."

"And? How was it?"

"It was...well, it was a little awkward, but I think that's just because I haven't kissed anyone else before." She looks at herself in the mirror. "Oh, gosh, I didn't even put on lip balm or anything."

"I'm sure he didn't mind, Katie." I giggle. "Plus, I'd be very surprised if that wasn't Floyd's first kiss, too." I smile at her. "I'm happy for you."

"Eek! Me, too. Thanks." She grins, her metal braces sparkling in the bathroom's bright light. "I just had to step away for a minute. It was all so much. How's it going with Jensen?"

"Good, so far."

"Well, I think he likes you. So that's all that matters."

"Yeah, thanks, Katie." I nod at the door. "You better get back to the theater. Floyd's going to worry something's wrong."

"Oh, gosh! Okay, yes." She pauses at the door. "Aren't you coming?"

"I'm going to freshen up for a second. It's okay. Go on back. I'm fine."

"You sure?"

"Yes." I laugh. "Go!"

She lets out one more joyful squeal before disappearing.

When the bathroom door shuts and I'm alone with my thoughts, I let out a long sigh and turn on the water. The cool liquid feels refreshing against my skin as I splash it onto my face. I stare into the mirror like I'm seeing myself for the first time. The thoughts of my mother, the Formulists, and Voidweavers start buzzing around my head like angry hornets.

And then they're replaced by fright.

The bathroom door opens, and Scythe is standing mere feet from me. The black strands from his bangs fall over his eye, and a wry smirk is spread across his ashen face.

"Hey, Genevieve."

I falter before finding the words. "Jensen is in the movie theater. He'll know something's wrong if I don't come back, and he'll—"

"He'll what?" Scythe sneers with a wolfish grin, flaunting his dazzling white teeth. "It would only take me a second to kill you." Like falling icicles, his blue eyes are piercing. "Jensen can't save you."

I take a step backwards, unsure what to do. I catch my reflection in the mirror and see that my hands are trembling.

"Please don't hurt me." My voice cracks. "Please."

Scythe's hard face washes away into concern.

He frowns. "Are you really that afraid of me? I'm not going to hurt you. I'm only joking."

I back up until I feel myself hugging the wall.

"Wh-why should I-I believe you?"

He steps closer to me, and I squeeze my eyes shut, hoping against all odds that this is a nightmare. But I know it isn't. I'm trapped, with nowhere to go and no one to help.

"I'm on your side, Genevieve." Scythe's lips are mere inches from my ear, and his breath is cool against my skin.

I feel a chill emanating from his body, and I taste his frostbitten breath as I inhale deeply. The air is cold within my lungs, and the image of a winter's snow emerges in my head. I can't help but shiver.

Within seconds, I feel him move away, and I open my eyes. He's now standing near the door.

"Maybe that will change your mind." He gestures to something he placed on the counter. "I'll see you around."

And then he's gone.

Next to the sink lays a piece of paper, worn and folded. With my trembling hand, I reach out and grab it, flip it around to reveal the other side. I recognize my mother's handwriting. My heart beats a thousand miles an hour as I read the words. I drop towards the floor, resting my hands on my knees to keep me steady. I inhale deeply, trying to clear my mind from the thick fog that has turned my brain to mush.

I read the paper again.

And again.

What is happening! Genevieve, what is happening.

My mind is swirling. I can't catch my breath. I need to—

"Genevieve!" Jensen says, as I crash into his chest, almost knocking the two of us to the floor.

I hadn't even realized I'd rushed back out of the bathroom and into the lobby.

"Whoa! Slow down." He grabs my shoulders to steady my body.

I raise my head to meet his gaze, and see panic strewn across his face.

"Are you okay? What happened?"

"I'm fine." I try to catch my breath. "I just…I didn't feel well. I'm sorry."

I look around the lobby, but see no sign of Scythe.

Jensen frowns. "You were gone for quite a while. I was afraid something was wrong."

I shake my head. "No. But I think I'd like to go home. Would you mind driving me?"

"Of course not." He grabs my hand as we begin walking towards the exit.

"Are you going to tell me what's going on?" Jensen says, as we pull into my driveway.

I haven't said anything since we left the mall. I only texted Katie to tell her we were leaving.

"Do you promise you won't get mad?" I say.

He raises his eyebrows. "I don't know what you could have done to make me mad at you. But okay."

I groan. "Just…just remember I'm okay now, yeah?"

"Genevieve. Please tell me."

"Scythe was at the theater." I speak quickly. "But he didn't hurt me. I was scared at first, yes, but then he just gave me this and left." I pull the piece of paper out of my pocket.

Jensen's eyes are dark, and I can see his face eclipsed with worry. His lips are taut as he takes the paper from me and unfolds it. We sit in silence as he reads.

"He gave this to you?" He flips over the paper. "Without any explanation?"

I shrug. "I think he was trying to tell me that he isn't one of the bad guys."

Jensen shakes his head. "Genevieve." He inhales deeply. "Genevieve, you are lucky you're alive. What if he *had* hurt you? Damnit!" He slaps the steering wheel with his hand. "I should have been there."

"Hey, it's okay, Jensen. *I'm* okay." I reach out and touch his shoulder.

His face is still sullen, stoic as he stares ahead.

"You couldn't have known he was going to be there."

"But I should have." He shakes his head. "I'm supposed to be protecting you."

"You're doing the best you can."

He scoffs. "Me *doing the best I can* isn't good enough."

An uncomfortable silence fills the Jeep.

"Why do you think Scythe gave that to me?"

"I don't know. I don't even know what it means."

Jensen reaches into the backseat to pull out a book and hand it to me. Its binding is red leather, and embroidered across the cover in gold etching is its title—*War and Lore: A Complete Review of the History of Formulists.*

"This book contains everything you could ever want to know about Banewind and the Formulists." He hands the piece of paper back to me. "Maybe you can find something in there to explain this. I can't recall, but I'll ask Sadie about it."

I run my hand over the cover, the book's weight heavy in my lap.

"Thank you," I whisper, and look at Jensen, his eyes still warm and inviting.

We lean closer to each other.

And then his lips are pressed against mine.

My world explodes into a blinding light, bursting forth an uncontrollable amount of excitement as I realize what's happening. My heart can no longer contain itself, and I feel it lurch into my throat as his lips press even harder. They are warm, soft, and full.

Within seconds, his tongue tickles along my lower lip, and I cringe in my chair, feeling my body tense as his every motion winds me tighter like a wind-up doll. I don't know how much more I'll be able to endure before I unravel at the seams, exposing myself to him.

He pulls away, leaving me with his sweet taste coating my lips. I open my eyes and stare blankly at him, my mind devoid of logic.

"Sadie and I will make sure to keep an eye on things tonight. I'll talk to you tomorrow. Call me for *anything*."

"Okay," I whisper. "Good night, Jensen." I grab the book and depart from the Jeep. *What a night.*

"Jeannie? Is that you?" I hear my dad say, as I enter the house.

"Hey, Dad. Yeah, I'm home."

He's sitting in front of the TV with a bowl of popcorn.

"Enjoying yourself?" I say.

"Couldn't ask for anything more." He smiles at me as he shovels a handful into his mouth. "You want to come join me? I have the ballgame on."

"No, thanks. I don't feel well. I left the movie early." I rub my stomach. "I think I just have a twenty-four-hour bug or something."

"Who drove you home?" His focus is still glued to the TV.

"The boy I went out with."

He turns to look at me with raised eyebrows.

"Oh, yeah? How did that go? You have a nice time with him?" He grins. "Or is that the reason you're *sick*?"

"Oh, no! No, seriously, I had a great time with him. I wasn't ditching him or anything. In fact, I think I'd like to go out with him again."

He wipes his hands off on a napkin. "Really? Well, that's great, Jeannie. You'll have to let me meet him soon." He takes a swig of beer. "I'm guessing you're heading to bed, then?"

"Yeah. Just wanted to say good night." I fake a yawn. "Some sleep will do me well."

"Okay. Good night, honey. I'll see you in the morning."

When I reach my room, I sit at my desk and turn on the lamp to see the photographs I found the other day staring back at me, taunting me with their mystery. I place the book next to them, along with the Blazing Vision talisman, and pull out the piece of paper Scythe gave me. I read the words on the note once more.

I know you always felt I favored him, and for that I'm sorry. But I can't kill him. He's too far gone, corrupted by Gresalmur, and more powerful than I could have imagined. Not even Lura's Light can stop him now.

But I can still make things right with the Binding Spell.

No matter what happens, no matter the outcome, don't follow me.

Protect Genevieve. Remind her always how much I love her. And remember how much I love you.

Be good, baby brother.

—Addisyn

After rereading my mother's words several more

times, I turn off the light and crawl into bed, an uneasy feeling sloshing around in my stomach.

Not only am I unfamiliar with words like *Gresalmur* or *Binding Spell*, but the worst of it all is *baby brother*.

Especially when I've grown up my entire life thinking I never had an uncle.

9

AUDIENCE

"ENTER," the woman with the bird skull adorning her head calls out, as the knock's echo dissipates around the circular room.

She stands at the other side of a dark pool, its waters reflecting the violet lights shining from the dome-shaped ceiling. The walls are lined with purple tapestries, embroidered into each of them a black helmet with two curving horns that cross each other, cradling a swirling vortex—the Voidweavers' insignia.

A mechanical *hiss* releases as the steel door rises, revealing two Voidweaver soldiers dressed in black suits, and an elderly man in between them. His arms are extended outward, and a bright pink light encompasses his wrists, keeping his hands cuffed together. The guards push into his back, and he stumbles forward on his bare feet, balancing himself to avoid toppling over into the pool's murky waters.

"You may leave us." The woman with the bird skull turns around to glare at the old man with her glowing amethyst eyes. "And go inform Commander Starmantle that I wish to speak with him."

The steel door slowly lowers as they depart, leaving the woman alone in the chamber with the frail man. They stand in silence.

"Mengurion Maldridge." Her purple cape flows down her back, barely brushing the floor. "So you know who I am?"

"I do, yes." His white beard flows down his chest, stopping at the top of his waist. "But tell me, please. What do you prefer I address you as?"

"You may call me the Dark Lady." Her words are hollow and carry an echo, hanging in the air with a chilling aura. "The name I have now come to embrace. The name the foolish inhabitants of Banewind have bestowed upon me without even realizing the complexity of my nature." Her red lips part into a wry smile. "No need for those, is there?" She flicks her gloved hand at Maldridge, and the pink handcuffs dissipate.

He rubs his wrists. "I will do nothing foolish. You have my word. I'm aware of the situation. And even so, I know my own limitations in my old age."

He stands there in his beige robe, tattered and torn. His long white hair is darkened by dirt, unkempt and disheveled.

"I was wondering if you'd speak with me."

"I debated on the necessity of seeing you, Maldridge. Quite frankly, I don't see a need. However, given our history, I felt it was still warranted." She inhales deeply. "Although, I already know it is futile in seeking any information from you."

"Well, you got what you wanted from me already. Do I need to even ask if you plan on keeping me alive?"

Six stone posts surround the pool, with silver claws carved into the top of each one. They each hold a crystal orb, and only one of them illuminates a dazzling green. The remainder are empty and unlit.

The Dark Lady moves forward and extends her hand to tap her fingers against the green glow.

"I was worried obtaining Gresalmur's Staff from you would be an arduous task." She chuckles. "But I had more friends in Quam'Naldon than I realized. There are many, many people who wish to see the Void King's return."

"There is no doubt your reach extends far, yes." Maldridge shakes his head. "But even so, there are plenty who will rise up against your cause. They've succeeded in the past, and they'll do so again. Addisyn DeWinter—"

"Spare me, Maldridge. Addisyn DeWinter only delayed the inevitable. I know you're smart enough to see that. She might have stopped the Voidweavers from unleashing the Darkness, but Ic'thyl still waits." The Dark Lady looks up at the tapestries. "I hear him, you know. I hear his voice, his whispers in my ear. Banewind's existence rests on such a taut string. It won't take much to," she snaps her fingers, "break it."

"I understand you believe this." Maldridge rubs his beard. "But you wouldn't be speaking to me right now if you weren't afraid. Addisyn's daughter lives. And so, too, then does the possibility of reviving the Holy Guardian. Lura's Light has been a staple to our people, and if they know it's still there, that it's only been stifled for the last decade..." his eyes widen as he smiles, "...well, then the chance that you fail is still very real."

The Dark Lady throws her hand at Maldridge, and a black beam jets across the room, smashing into his chest. He cries out as he's tossed against the steel door, and falls to the ground with a *thud!*

"Foolish mage, you think yourself so wise," the Dark

Lady snarls. "Paladins. Holy Magic. Light. Love. None of it matters. Have you learned nothing during your years of living? Why must you squander them?"

Maldridge rises to his knees, groaning as he takes to his feet.

"I've seen a lot through these old eyes." He shakes his head. "You aren't the first to be corrupted by dark magic, and you certainly won't be the last."

"Hmph." The Dark Lady stares down at the pool. "Felyx Crimsley helped build this pool. Do you remember?" She bends down and removes one of her gloves to let her fingers slip through the waters. "I believe he said something similar, about being *corrupted*. It's such a subjective term, really. Corruption merely depends on what side of the looking glass you're on."

A loud knock reverberates through the room as the door behind Maldridge opens once more.

"Dark Lady, you wanted to see me?" A young man enters the room.

His body is clad in black armor, but his white eyes shine through his helmet.

"Yes, Commander Starmantle." She stares at Maldridge. "I was going to instruct you to kill Magister Maldridge here...but I've changed my mind. I think we could still have some fun together." She places her glove back on her hand, turning away from the two men. "Take him back to his cell."

"Of course." He grabs Maldridge by the arm and leads him away.

"Good to see you again, old friend," the Dark Lady calls, as the door shuts, locking her away once more to be alone in her thoughts.

Maldridge steps back into his cell.

"I'm sorry." The young knight punches a number into the keypad, and a pink barrier appears, separating the old mage from him. "I didn't know she was calling for you."

"No apologies, Kingston," Maldridge says. "I am aware of the situation's graveness. I realize my life could soon be coming to an end."

Kingston looks around to make sure no one is near him in the Prison Ward.

"I did what you asked me to do," he says. " I found the necklace, and I gave it to Scythe. It was where you said it would be."

"So they didn't destroy all of my home?" Maldridge smiles weakly. "That's good to know. Thank you."

"The Magician and Valkryn are planning to bring the girl here soon. I'm not sure how they'll get her to Banewind, but they're close. Is there anything else I need to do?"

"Casius gave you the portal key, correct?"

Kingston nods.

"Good. You must make sure you continue to keep an eye on Genevieve. Do what you can to keep her safe. I understand it is a dire situation and challenging to do, given your relations with the Voidweavers and Valkryn. But if Genevieve comes to Banewind alone, this will not work. She needs to be with Scythe."

"I understand," Kingston says. "I'll do what I can. In the meantime, is there anything I can get you?"

"Peace of mind would be nice." Maldridge smiles. "If I don't make it—"

"Magister, you'll—"

Maldridge raises his hand. "If I don't make it, you must inform Gerard Saint Clair about everything I told you. He'll help you out as much as I can."

"There's no need for that. You'll be safe. I gave Casius my word that I would keep you alive. You'll get out of here soon. I promise."

A distant sound emerges as several soldiers enter the Prison Ward.

"Go now, Kingston," Maldridge says. "Remember. Keep her away from Banewind until she's here with Scythe. It's the only way this will work."

Kingston gives one final nod before turning away from Maldridge and disappearing down the vast prison's hall.

10

BOOKS & NOTES

ONCE AGAIN, I'M IN MY WHITE BALLGOWN, watching as my Prince Charming beckons for me from the bottom of the staircase. And once again, I rush toward him only to find myself trapped on a never-ending set of stairs. The lights are dimming, the people are fading, and he's disappearing as the sound of rolling thunder gets louder and louder. I'm screaming, but I can't hear myself. There is heat all around me. Flames and flashes illuminate the darkness. I stumble over my dress, tearing the train in two. I lose my footing. I'm falling now.

Down. Down. Down.

My eyes snap open.

A thin beam of light is sneaking past the curtains and illuminating half my bed. I sit up and look at the clock—10:30 a.m. I lean over and see that my phone has a text message from Jensen.

I won't be in town this weekend. I had an emergency meeting with the Council. If you need anything, call Sadie. Here's her number. I'll talk to you soon.

"Great." I'm curious what he would qualify as an *emergency.*

I see my mother's note and pick it up, wondering if that has anything to do with what's going on. The Formulist book sits next to it on the desk.

My cell phone vibrates, and I look down to see another text, this time from Katie.

How are you feeling this morning? Everything okay?

I look back at the Formulist book.

And then a thought pops into my head.

Don't do it. Genevieve, don't do it.

I dial Katie's number.

"Hey," I say. "You want to go to the library with me?"

It only takes me five minutes to get there, and luckily it's not too crowded inside. The library isn't that big of a place, but it was remodeled a couple years ago, so everything is in great condition. The tables are spacious, the furniture is comfy, and the artwork throughout the building gives off an inviting feeling—from art projects done by our local elementary schools, to replicated sculptures and paintings from all sorts of famous artists across history. My favorite is *Las Meninas* by Diego Velázquez.

I set down my backpack at an empty table near the fiction section, a place I've frequented countless times before. My home away from home.

I pull out the Formulist book as Katie arrives.

"Hey." She sets down her own textbooks on the table. "I'm glad you called me, I was worried about you last night after the movie."

"I know. I'm sorry I left like that. Did you and Floyd have a good time?"

"We did." Her cheeks blush. "He asked me out on another date, and this time it'll just be the two of us."

"Oh, thank goodness." I laugh. "But that doesn't mean we can't do more double dates in the future."

"Absolutely." Her smile widens. "What about you and Jensen?"

I take a deep breath, preparing what I'm about to say to her as I look around to make sure we're not being overheard.

"Katie, I need to tell you something. And you're gonna want to make sure you're seated."

"So..." I say, after I finish telling her about the Voidweavers.

After the initial shock of divulging the secret of the Formulists and Banewind to Katie, it only took her a few minutes to regain composure so I could catch her up on everything else. Besides a few gasps, cries, and moments where I felt she might lose consciousness, she appeared to handle everything fairly well as I brought her up to speed on the rollercoaster that was now my life.

"What do you think?"

Her mouth gaping open is answer enough for me.

"Genevieve." The color to her face is finally starting to return. "Genevieve, what the hell?"

"I know. I really didn't believe it at first, either. But," I pull my mother's note from my backpack and hand it to her, "this was the note Scythe gave me yesterday at the theater. And here are the pictures from the funeral." I slide them across the table. "I'm so sorry I've been acting weird the last couple days. I wanted to tell you sooner, but I didn't even have my own head wrapped around any of it." I sigh. "And now, with realizing my dad might know about it, and that I could have some uncle out there in Banewind,"

I slap my hand against the Formulist book, "let alone this thing Jensen gave me," I bite my lip, "I just...I couldn't keep it from you any longer. You're my best friend. We tell each other *everything*."

Katie scans the photos, flipping through them with the same look of disbelief I'm sure I had when I found them.

She takes off her glasses and rubs her eyes, shaking her head.

"I..." She closes her eyes and inhales. "I can't believe you've been dealing with all this on your own." She puts her glasses back on and reaches across the table to grab my hands. "Genevieve, I am so happy that you told me. You have nothing to apologize for." She pulls back and opens the Formulist book, paging through the text. "This is...I don't even have a word to describe what I'm feeling."

"Inconceivable?"

"Extraordinary! To know that another *world* exists? That magic is *real*? Genevieve, this is the stuff you and I have dreamed of since we were children. All those fairytale slumber parties, the midnight book releases, the trips to Disney World." She catches her breath. "It's all *real!*"

"You're making it sound nicer than it is. Slumber parties and Disney trips didn't encompass the Voidweavers trying to destroy the world." I frown. "They didn't involve the Void King killing my mother."

"I know. You're right. I'm sorry. But what I'm saying is that *of course* I believe you. And *of course* I'm here to help you in whatever way you need."

"Thank you." I'm on the brink of tears.

To have such a best friend as her, someone I can depend on no matter what, who always has my back, who understands me for who I really am...

"I love you so much."

"And I love you, too." She squeezes my hand again. "So what now?"

"I don't know." I clear my throat, brushing away the moisture from the corner of my eyes. "There's not really any plan." I glance at the Formulist book.

"The woman you saw at the mall...Ilona, right?"

"Mhm."

"She didn't give you any guidance on what to do next?"

"No." I sigh, pulling out the talisman she gave me. "I didn't even tell Jensen about her, with everything else on my mind." I hand Katie the coin with the Blazing Vision's eye staring back at me. "I was just going to spend some time reading the Formulist book, and touch base with Jensen and Sadie after the weekend."

"Hmm." Katie examines the metal object, turning it over in her fingers, before handing it back. "Well, how can I help?"

"I don't think I have enough mental stamina to learn anything more about the Formulists at the moment." I slide the book to her. "Would you like to look through this over the weekend? Jensen didn't seem too optimistic that there'd be anything in it to help us immediately. But of course, we need to learn more about Banewind's history." I sigh. "I just want a couple days to collect myself."

"Absolutely!" Her eyes gleam with excitement. "You don't think he'd mind if I borrow it?"

I laugh. "Well, he doesn't even know I told you, so I'm not sure how he'll feel about that. But that can wait. Like I said, he isn't even in town right now."

"So he went back to Banewind? To meet with the Council of the Formulists?"

I shrug. "I guess so. He didn't specify."

"Well, I'd be more than honored to read this. I'll let you know if I find out anything interesting."

"Perfect. I think I'm going to go home and take a nap. I need it."

We sit there in silence for a few minutes, before leaving, and I think about how nice it is to have someone I can just be alone with, comfortably, without having to speak.

Everyone could use a Katie in her life.

I don't know what I'd do without her.

The remainder of the weekend passes innocently enough. I go to bed early and wake up late the next morning. I take most of the day to finish my homework assignments, a task I find challenging as my mind constantly attempts to redirect me back to the Formulists.

I spend Sunday evening in front of the TV with my family. Danny is playing videos games, and my dad is busy getting his class's syllabus ready for the start of his school next week.

I still don't want to bring this up to him. Not yet, anyway.

The next morning, I again pick Katie up from her house. As she approaches the car, I see her carrying the Formulist book.

"Hey." I'm eyeing the large text. "How's it going?"

"I can't stop reading this." Katie rubs her fingers against the golden letters, and I see several sticky notes peeking from the pages. "It's absolutely fascinating."

"Have you learned anything more?" I pull out of the driveway. "Is...my mother mentioned in it?"

"Not directly, no. They do have a section on the

Holy Guardians, but it mostly just talks about the centuries of work they've done to protect Banewind." Katie laughs. "Your ancestors must have been really, really cool, Jeannie. Especially if they were descendants of this goddess Lura."

"Too bad I never knew about them until now." I groan. "What about the Binding Spell?"

"No. But I do think I know what kind of magic it's referring to. There's another group of Formulists known as the Jintüroo, who are able to manipulate the earth with their powers. Actually, the history suggests that they're one of the oldest groups in Banewind, perhaps the people that were living there before the connection to our world was even created." Katie has the book open in her lap, and is scouring various passages. "According to the book, *The Jintüroo are masters of manipulating earth and its natural elements. They are thought to be responsible for numerous catastrophic events throughout Banewind. From earthquakes to eruptions to avalanches, the magnitude of their powers knows no limits. As well as with the ability to create, form, and bind, the Jintüroo are a fierce and formidable group that prefer the seclusion and isolation of their destitute home in the far west of the Wastelands.*"

"Wastelands?" I say.

"One of the territories in Banewind. But do you hear that? The ability to *bind?*" Katie squeals. "I think we're on to something."

"Yeah, that sounds possible. Anything else?"

I know I'm getting my hopes up, but I just wish there was something in the book that mentioned my mother, uncle, or anything else that might answer some of my questions.

Katie shrugs. "There's tons of stuff in here, including lots of passages already highlighted, and some notes scribbled in the margins. But nothing pertinent to what you're looking for, I don't think. But don't worry. We still have tons of time to digest this."

"Right." Not sure if I believe that. "We'll just keep looking."

When I arrive at school, Katie runs off to the library before class to keep reading, while I head to my locker. I take off the lock and pull open the door. A note flutters down to the floor.

My heart skips a beat as I unfold it to read its contents.

Genevieve,

Meet me at your car.

—Scythe

I turn around, half-expecting him to be standing there waiting for me, as a shiver runs down my spine.

What could he have to tell you, Genevieve?

"Crap." I think about the last time I saw Scythe...the note he gave me.

I take out my phone and call Jensen.

Straight to voicemail.

Genevieve, think! You're a smart girl.

I could go tell Sadie about this and see what she says, but my guess is that she won't want me to meet him. And although we *think* Scythe is dangerous, he hasn't hurt me. And he did give me my mother's note.

I could also text Katie and tell her what's going on. But then I might be putting her in danger. It's probably bad enough I told her about the Formulists.

You're at school. Even if he were going to hurt you, he wouldn't do it here, would he?

But I don't know that for sure. It's a gamble...and a high-risk one. But could the benefit outweigh it?

Crap.

Crap. Crap. Crap!

I take a deep breath and head for the parking lot. As I approach my car, I see Scythe standing next to the passenger door. A smile widens across his face when he sees me.

"I wasn't sure that would work." He grins.

"What do you want?" I fold my hands across my chest. "I have to get going to class."

He chuckles. "You're cute when you're trying to be all tough."

My face flushes. I stand there, my gaze locked on him. His black silky hair is tussled by the wind.

"Where did you get that note from my mother?" I still keep my distance.

He frowns. "I can't tell you that. Sorry." He steps towards me. "But I can assure you that it was from someone who cares about your mother." He shifts on his feet. "What if I told you that she isn't dead?"

My stomach flips upside down.

"That's not funny." My voice cracks. "That is *not* funny."

"I agree, it's not." His face is expressionless. "And it's even less funny that you don't know about it already."

"My mother is dead," I hiss. "Has been for years." I feel tears welting up.

I was not expecting to have this conversation. How twisted can this boy be?

He sighs and shakes his head. "The truth isn't always what it seems. You know that."

"Get away from me." I back up. "Get away from me

and leave me alone!" I turn back towards the school.

"Wait!" Scythe's voice recoils through my ears. "Here." He reaches into his pocket and pulls out a golden pendant. "Do you recognize this?"

I hesitate before stepping forward and reaching out to grab the necklace he's extending to me.

"This was my mother's." I gasp and turn the spherical pendant over.

There are three sapphires embedded into the gold.

"How do you have this?" I look him in the eyes. "Who gave this to you?"

"I told you, I can't say. I promised I wouldn't. But isn't that enough to show you I'm not one of the bad guys?"

We stand there in silence. In the distance, I hear the bell sound for first period.

He looks at me with his piercing blue eyes once more before turning away toward the surrounding woods.

"I'll be at the cemetery at eleven o'clock tonight, waiting for you. I'll show you I'm not wrong." He pauses and looks back over his shoulder at me. "I'll wait for one hour."

I open my mouth to say something, but no words come out.

"Just get to class, Genevieve," he calls from the forest's edge.

"Genevieve, you're late," Sadie says, as I enter the classroom.

I must still look shaken, because I see worry splash across her face.

"Are you okay, dear?"

"I'm fine." I take my seat next to Katie. "I'm sorry for

being late. It won't happen again."

I can feel Katie looking at me, but I don't return the gaze. I just want to sit here alone in my own thoughts. But I can't think. I'm numb. Lost in...nothing.

The bell to end first period rings.

"Genevieve, a word?" Sadie calls, as I'm about to leave the classroom.

Katie stands at the door for me, but I motion for her to go on. I bite my lip as I walk over to Sadie's desk.

She waits for everyone to clear out of the room.

"Are you okay? Jensen told me what happened with Scythe. And the note from your mother." She pushes her blonde hair back behind her ears. "How are you feeling?"

"I'm not sure. Sadie, do you think my mother could still be alive?"

"What? Genevieve, what on earth makes you ask that?"

"The note Scythe left. Maybe it was a clue." I have my one hand in my jean pocket, and can feel the necklace cold against my skin.

Sadie sighs. "I don't know Scythe's motive behind giving you that note. But if your mother were still alive..." she smiles weakly, "...well, I would like to think she would have let me know. Somehow, anyway."

"Did you know she had a brother?"

Sadie looks away. "I did. He was a good man. His name was Felyx. But eventually he and your mother lost touch." She sighs. "It happens, even with the best of families."

The bell for the next period rings.

"Oh, shoot. I'm sorry I've kept you from being on time. Jensen should be back tonight. In the meantime, if you need anything, please let me know."

"Thanks, Sadie." I turn to leave the room, but pause at the door. "Sadie?" I look back at her. "Are you really even a teacher? Or did you and Jensen just do all this as a cover up to look out for me?"

"Oh, Genevieve." She laughs. "I guess that's a fair question. Yes, I am an instructor at the Academy, back in Banewind. Did Jensen mention our school to you?"

"Kinda."

"The Formulists' Institution of Academia and Educational Pursuit, or the Academy, is a prestigious school located in Banewind's capital city, Quam'Naldon. Most children attend the Academy through their younger years, usually completing their studies by the age of eighteen. After that, they continue on to more advanced studies or trade skills if they wish. There's a plethora of options to choose from."

"What do you teach?"

"I'm an instructor in Ice Magic, as well as Beast Elementology. I'm sure it won't surprise you to hear there are tons of different creatures that inhabit our world, and I've always been fond of animals, so I made my passion into a career."

"I guess that overlays with biology."

Sadie smiles. "My sister, Roselia—Jensen's mother— is director of the Biological, Magical, and Behavioral Department at the Academy. It was her idea to have Jensen and I come here to protect you while things were getting sorted out with the Voidweavers. It's much easier for the director of a department to finagle my absence than anyone else's." She glances at the clock. "Okay, you really must be off to class. Here." She takes her pen and scribbles it across a piece of paper. "An excuse for your tardiness. Have a good day, Miss DeWinter."

Once I leave the room, I put the excuse slip into my pocket and feel the pendant of my mother's necklace. I pull it out and place it around my neck, realizing that I still know nothing about Banewind.

When I arrive home, I sequester myself in my room, trying to focus on my homework. I watch the clock slowly tick by as I decide on what to do about Scythe. My head is still pounding, so I skip dinner and take some Tylenol. Maybe if I lie down for a little bit, I'll feel better.

I dream about my mother. I see her face smiling at me. Hear her bright voice and her charming laugh. She looks so happy.

And then she's terrified.

She's trapped inside a coffin. She can't breathe. I watch her choking, gasping for air. Her eyes roll back, and foam rises out of her mouth. She convulses. The wooden box around her is growing tighter and tighter. I hear her scream. Louder. Louder. Louder!

I snap my eyes open, springing up in bed. The clock reads quarter to eleven.

"Screw this." I throw on my purple hoodie and pull out my phone to dial Jensen's number. *Please pick up. Please pick up.*

"Genevieve?" His warm voice greets me.

I breathe a sigh of relief. "I'm so happy you answered."

"I literally just got back. What's wrong? Are you okay?"

"I need you to come pick me up. But no questions until we're together."

"Now?"

"Yes. I'm at my house. My family is asleep, and I

don't want to risk waking them up by starting my car."

"Okay, I'm on my way. See you soon."

I tiptoe through the darkened house. When I reach the kitchen, I see a flashlight sitting in the nearby cubby and decide to take it. I shove it into my hoodie pocket and disappear outside.

A few minutes later, Jensen pulls onto the street. I look back at my house before getting into the Jeep. An odd feeling hangs in the air, filling me with uncertainty.

And then we're driving through the starlit night.

11

THE CEMETERY

I HAVEN'T BEEN TO THE CEMETERY in a long time. When I was little, I remember coming to visit my mother's resting place every week. My father and I would first go to the florist and buy her favorite flowers, tiger lilies, to place inside the mausoleum. It was always so cold and quiet inside the structure, and I can remember feeling scared the first few times I visited her.

Dad had the mausoleum constructed so the rest of the family could be placed inside there along Mom. But even now, I think of how lonely it must be. Of course, that doesn't matter to the inhabitants, does it?

We pull up to the main entrance. The iron-barred gates are shut tight with a padlock, and the grounds are pitch dark.

Jensen turns off the engine.

"Are you sure about this?" He's wearing his red cloak, and rolls up the sleeves.

"No. But I need to find out what else Scythe knows."

"You know this could be a trap." Jensen gets out of the car. "As far as we're aware, Scythe is still with the Voidweavers."

"I know." I look down at my mother's pendant hanging around my neck, and take the golden sphere in between my fingers. "But there's something we're missing here, Jensen. He's given me both a letter and a necklace from my mother." I sigh. "That's gotta say something."

"You're right." He nods, walking over to the gate.

I follow him out of the car.

"Well, let's find out what we can." He picks up the padlock as his hands glow fiery orange, melting the metal into mush.

Although I might be getting used to the idea of magic, it doesn't stop my heart from beating in double-time.

He pulls on the gate, and it slowly creaks open.

"Give me your flashlight." He reaches out towards me. "And hold my hand, please."

I don't like admitting it, but even in this situation, I feel starstruck the moment I grab hold of his warm hand. I wrap my fingers around his, following close to his side as he leads the way into the cemetery. The flashlight only illuminates a few feet in front of us, but even so, I know where to direct him.

"Go left, Jensen. No, *left*," I whisper. "Geez, you would think you'd have a better sense of direction after all the traveling you do."

He chuckles. "Oh, I'm sorry, Genevieve. Forgive me for trying to avoid the gravestones sticking out of the ground. I'm a mage, not a ghost."

"Okay, it should be right over there. Hmm. I don't know. This place looks so different at night. Uh...yes. Yep. There. Right over there." I point to the stone structure in front of us. "That's it."

"Looks like somebody is already here." Jensen's hand

tenses in mine as he shines the light over the opened metal door.

"I'm sure it's Scythe." I bite my lip. "I didn't tell him you were coming, you know."

"Well, he'll have to get over it."

We approach the mausoleum. The flashlight's beam catches on the stone, and I can see the intricate carvings covering the monument's exterior. A marble cross sits atop the roof, reflecting the dim moonlight.

"I guess we're about to find out if we can really trust Scythe." Jensen frowns at me. "If anything happens, just get yourself to safety, okay?"

I enter after him and see Scythe sitting in the back corner, with a flashlight pointed at us. Above him, on the stone mantle, rests a bouquet of dead flowers in a glass vase left from years ago.

"How did I know you'd bring Jensen?" Scythe's words echo past my ears. "That kinda hurts you don't trust me."

"You're lucky we're even here," Jensen spews.

"Yeah, well, whatever." Scythe walks over to the crypt where my mother's casket rests. "This is it, right?"

I take the flashlight from Jensen and shine it on the writing etched into the marble plaque.

ADDISYN ELIZABETH DEWINTER
BELOVED MOTHER AND WIFE
MARCH 19TH, 1978 – NOVEMBER 1ST, 2012

A lump swells in the back of my throat.

"What if you're wrong?" I whisper, feeling the tears forming, and turn to Scythe with pleading eyes. "What if she is still in there?"

"I don't think she is, Genevieve," Scythe says, his words softer than before. "But..."

My mother's warm face emerges in my mind. Her bright blue eyes, caring smile. Her blonde hair gently blowing in the summer's breeze. If there is any chance that she's still alive...I need to know.

I grasp her necklace once more.

"Let's do it." I sound more confident than I feel.

Scythe nods. "Right, then."

"I'll handle this," Jensen growls.

He steps forward as he pushes Scythe out of the way. His fingers burn through the marble as he traces along the plaque's border. I watch as the sparks jump out into the darkness.

"Come here and grab this end," Jensen says to Scythe, as his flames cut through the final piece of stone.

Scythe places his flashlight on the mantle next to the vase before approaching Jensen. The plaque falters before falling forward into their hands.

"It's heavy." Scythe groans, stumbling backward from the marble's weight. "You okay?"

"Fine." Jensen lowers the plaque to the ground, and it hits the floor with a soft *thud*.

I turn my flashlight into the crypt and see my mother's oak casket, preserved perfectly behind the stone wall.

"Genevieve, why don't you grab the middle?" Scythe motions to the handle. "I can take this end, and Jensen that one." He eyes Jensen with caution. "You cool with that?"

"Just be careful, Genevieve. We all pull on the count of three. Ready?"

I position myself on the handle and nod at Jensen.

"Okay. One. Two. Three!"

The casket resists at first, but then lunges forward, propelling me backwards across the mausoleum. I trip over the marble plaque and lose my grip, watching in horror as the casket plummets to the ground.

CRAAAAAAASH!

"Noooo!" I scream, over the thundering roar that reverberates around the mausoleum.

The room is now thick with dust, and I close my eyes, coughing as I inhale the stale air.

"Genevieve!" Jensen rushes to my side. "Are you all right?"

I'm leaning against the wall, staring blankly at the casket in front of me. The fall's force has caused the lid to spring open, revealing the box's contents.

Nothing.

"It's...it's empty," I whisper, then pick up the flashlight lying next to me, and take a step toward the casket.

The white-laced material lining the box looks brand-new.

"I don't...It can't..." *How could...and what does...I don't understand.*

"Genevieve," Jensen whispers.

I hear him step toward me.

All at once, I feel hot anger building inside me. My nostrils are flaring, my breathing rapid. I spin around and glare at Scythe, shining the flashlight in his face.

"Where is my mother?"

"What?" His eyes widen with surprise. "I told you, I don't—"

"You knew she wasn't dead. You knew the casket would be empty." My mind is blinded with rage. "How? How did you know, Scythe?"

"I...I..." He pulls his gaze away from mine.

"Scythe, how did you know?"

"Oh, come now, Miss DeWinter," says an unfamiliar voice. "You give the boy too much credit. He was only acting on what was told to him. He knows nothing more than that."

I turn around and see a tall, lanky man standing at the mausoleum's entrance. My flashlight's beam reflects off his orange trench coat, catching on the shine from his black boots. The matching orange, pointed hat he wears is skewed to the side, casting a dark shadow over his face.

"I appreciate your help in bringing the girl here, though, Scythe. I really do." He steps forward and grins wryly, flashing his stained teeth. "For a while I was concerned this wouldn't work. But you seem to have proved me wrong."

"You..." Jensen snarls at Scythe, his eyes irate with anger. "I knew you couldn't be trusted."

"What! Wait, no. I didn't do—"

"Shut up." Jensen's words are toxic. "Or I'll kill you right now."

"Oh, how exciting." The man chuckles and claps, then clears his throat. "But alas, now is not the time for you to kill Scythe. We have more...pressing matters to attend to. Wouldn't you agree?"

"Please!" Scythe says. "Let me explain. I didn't—"

The man flicks his hand, and a bright fiery ball rushes at Scythe, knocking him unconscious against the wall.

"There we are." The man moves closer to me. "Just the three of us to chat."

Jensen stands tense, his fists clenched at his side.

"Oh, please don't do anything foolish." The man points at me. "I would rather not have her watch you die. That would be quite traumatic."

"Let her go," Jensen says.

For the first time, I see that he's afraid.

"This isn't her fight. Please."

"Ah, but you see Mister Saint Clair. Both you and I know that isn't true." The man looks at me and gasps. "Oh! Why, my apologies, my dear. Where are my manners? I have neglected to introduce myself." The tip of his hat brushes against the floor as he bows low to the ground. "My name is Blaine Fortrunner." He gleams at me with his dark, beady eyes. "But I am known to most simply as the Magician."

"Genevieve, don't speak to him." Jensen keeps his gaze glued to the Magician. "Don't say a word. He's with the Voidweavers."

"Oh, Mister Saint Clair. How you offend me!" The Magician collapses his hands to his chest. "Don't you even want to hear what I have to say? You don't know what I've come for."

I look around the mausoleum, desperately trying to think of some way to get out of this situation.

"Your words do not interest me," Jensen growls. "The only thing I wish to hear is your corpse falling to the floor."

Think, Genevieve, think!

I see Scythe's flashlight sitting on the mantle. And the glass vase next to it.

"Mister Saint Clair, why do you defend a girl of whom you know nothing?" The Magician turns to face Jensen. "Forgive me if I'm mistaken, but isn't it true that your belief that the girl's a paladin is merely a...supposition?" He shakes his head. "That's an awfully big risk to take, wouldn't you say?"

The mantle is merely an arm's length away. If I can just time it right...

"If that's true, then why do the Voidweavers want

her?" Jensen says. "Why must you capture an innocent girl?"

"I am merely acting on the orders of the Dark Lady. And she presumes the girl to be a key—"

Whack!

I thrust the glass vase against the Magician's head, closing my eyes as the vessel shatters into pieces.

"Genevieve, run!" Jensen screams, over the cascading shards.

I lunge, but feel a skeleton-like hand wrap around my arm.

"You little wretch," the Magician snarls.

Fresh blood streams down the side of his face, dripping onto his orange trench coat.

"I'm going to make sure you suffer for—"

The mausoleum illuminates bright orange as a giant heatwave rolls over my head. I watch as Jensen's fireball slams into the Magician, tossing him aside like a ragdoll.

"Run!" Jensen screams again.

I don't need to be told a third time. I rush from the mausoleum and into the cemetery, feeling the night's wind lash across my face. My feet fly over the dampened ground, and I focus on nothing but the darkness that lies in front of me.

Run, run, run! Run! Don't stop. Don't look back. Don't slow down.

Wait. Look out!

The tombstone is mere inches from me. I jump and sail over it like a hurdle, losing my balance as I slam face first into the mud. I choke as the dirt flies into my mouth and lodges at the back of my throat. I splutter and cough, gasping for breath.

From behind, I hear an explosion. A column of orange fire splits the night sky. I watch in horror as it climbs high into the air, clawing at the stars.

I feel as though a knife has stabbed me in the stomach as I realize Jensen is still back there with the Magician.

"Jensen!" I scream, tears rushing down my face.

I pull myself up from the mud and stumble forward as the earth shakes beneath me.

"No, no, no!" I race back toward the fiery pillar.

The blood-red sky illuminates the entire cemetery, and each tombstone seems to shudder under the immense inferno.

Don't go back! Don't go back. You are going to die, Genevieve. Stop!

Several trees are now ablaze, and the black smoke billows into the air.

Stop, Genevieve! Stop.

No. I will not let him die. I will *not* let him die.

"Genevieve!" a woman's voice calls.

I stop dead in my tracks and turn toward the sound. But that's all I can do. It only takes a moment for the blinding light to immerse around me. I scream a blood-curdling shriek as I flail my arms, trying to orient myself. But there is no sense of dimension, no sense of time.

Within seconds, all goes silent.

I am alone.

12

THE COURT OF ANGUISH

I OPEN MY EYES AND STARE AT THE DARK SKY.

But it isn't the same fiery, night sky that cloaked the cemetery just moments before. Now the sky is blotched with stars, and wisps of gray clouds scatter across its length. A purple hue hangs in the air, casting an eerie glow over the surrounding land.

A bellowing roar cuts through the silence.

"I would suggest getting up if I were you," says someone nearby.

I gingerly rise to my feet. My mind is hazy, and I feel nauseous. Next to me is a young man draped in black armor. He grasps a sword, and his helmet has two sharp horns twisting into the air.

"Can I trust you to stay right here?" He points to the black platform we're standing on. "Can I?" he repeats, when I don't answer.

The roar rings out once more.

"Damnit." He runs off, but pauses and turns back towards me. "Please just stay here."

He disappears into the darkness.

Yes, I'm confused.

Obviously, I realize I am no longer in the cemetery. But I have no idea where I am.

Jagged rocks surround me like a canyon, and the only thing in this barren gorge is the black platform I'm standing on. Ahead of me lies the path that the young man just departed down.

"Crap." I try to keep myself from freaking out. "Crap, crap, crap."

I pull out my cell phone to call Jensen, but discover I have no service. Frustrated, I drop the phone back into my pocket and replay the recent events inside my head.

You escaped, and I'm sure Jensen did, too. But how did I end up here? I was running back to help Jensen, when...yes, I heard a woman's voice call my name. And that was it.

The distant sky explodes into a dazzling array of lights. And then screams echo all around me. My heart races once more.

I know that guy told me to stay here, but what the heck. I don't know him. Could this just be another ploy to try to kill me?

I'd rather not wait around to find out.

I take off down the winding path, guided by the bright colors that are exploding into the sky at a greater frequency than before. A screech resonates through the canyon, piercing my ears in a deafening tone.

More screams fill the night's void. The air has become thick, coating my nostrils with the pungent smell of burnt wood. I continue to rush down the twisting path, panicking as I start feeling trapped between the rocky walls. My breaths are shallow. My hair is sticking to my face.

I hear the sound of flames crackling nearby. More shouts emanate. I must be close to the source now.

The canyon gives way as I emerge into a new area.

My mouth opens to scream, but my voice is paralyzed with fear. In front of me is an enormous sprawling courtyard, littered with metal debris and flaming wooden carts, spouting their black smoke into the air. Several lifeless bodies lay in contorted positions, some even missing limbs. Rows of tents are ablaze in fire while their inhabitants scurry to escape. They scream in agony as the green flames lick their bodies, charring them to black ashes.

And in the courtyard's center stands a creature bellowing an earth-rattling roar. The humanoid beast towers high into the sky like a behemoth, spewing soot and fire from its nostrils and mouth. The head is shaped like that of a dragon, composed of blackened bone and a pair of twisting horns. Its eyes pierce across the courtyard like two burning ember coals, casting an iridescent glow on the ground beneath it.

The large, hulking body is consumed in green flames, and its arms are sprawled out to the side, spanning the length of several full-grown men. It rears its head back once more, rumbling out its bone-chilling call as it steps forward on its enormous, reptilian-like feet.

Oh, my God. I am frozen in place.

"You stupid girl!" A hand wraps around my arm and yanks me in its direction. "I told you to stay at the portal." The same man that had been on the black platform with me, is now pulling me across the courtyard. "What the hell is wrong with you?"

I'm still unable to find my voice. Several men have approached the creature's feet, and slash at them with swords and axes. A few yards back stands another group, and I watch in awe as their fireballs and ice bolts hurl towards the monster's chest and crash into it with a thunderous explosion.

"Look out!"

Before anyone can respond to the warning, the creature smashes its claws onto the ground. A monstrous wall of green flames sweeps across the courtyard like a tsunami, engulfing the remaining fighters. I watch in horror as their bodies disintegrate into nothing.

We're still running to the edge of the courtyard, when I'm pulled to a halt.

"Careful!" The man throws out his arm to catch me before I take another step.

The blood drains from my face as I realize there is nothing surrounding the courtyard but a black abyss. I'm balancing precariously on the edge.

"I...wha..."

"This time, will you *promise* me you'll stay here?" He motions to a nearby boulder.

All I can do is nod.

"Good." He pulls the sword from its sheath on his back.

His black armor reflects the flickering flames that now cover most of the courtyard. I can't make out his face behind the helmet, but his eyes are glowing white through the slits.

I clamor behind the boulder as soon as he turns and runs off towards the beast. I realize that he and I are the only ones still alive in the courtyard, and a sinking feeling in my stomach makes me fear that soon it might just be me.

"Don't worry. He knows what he's doing." A voice echoes from behind me.

My heart drops into my stomach as I spin around, half-expecting to see the Magician. But there's no one there.

"I prefer anonymity in situations such as these,"

says the disembodied voice. "My apologies. But I am more suited to the clandestine lifestyle than most. Ah, are you watching? Your friend is about to deal with this nuisance."

Still unable to identify the source of the voice, I turn my attention back towards the man. He's now standing in front of the monster, with his sword outstretched, pointing the tip at its fiery torso. He screams a loud cry as a bolt of black light bursts forth from the sword, piercing the monster's chest. It throws back its head and snarls, ejecting its fire high into the air. The black beam spreads across the monster, entangling its limbs like gnarled vines, as the embers rain down onto the courtyard.

Within moments, the blackness has sealed the monster, and it's frozen in place.

"Raggghhhhh!"

He plunges his sword into the monster's leg. As he pulls it out, the creature shatters into a thousand black pieces which clatter to the ground like a broken mirror.

The dying embers crackle their melancholy tune across the courtyard as the air slowly clears. He sheaths his sword and walks back towards me.

"That," he gestures over his shoulder, at the monster's remains, "was a Shadow Dredger." He shakes his head and sighs. "Unfortunately, the poor fool who conjured it had no idea what he was doing." He pulls off his helmet and grins at me. "Which, luckily for you, was the best thing that could have happened tonight."

I'm surprised to see that the face hiding under the helmet belongs to a young man who appears to be in his early twenties. His pale skin shines bright, like that of the sun reflecting off snow, and a glistening white hue glows around his eyes. His facial features are handsome, with high-set cheekbones and sharply defined jaw lines. But his thin, gray lips and pallid hair give him a sense of foreboding.

"Now..." he sighs, running his hand through his white hair, "...can we return to the topic of what a stupid girl you are?"

"That's insulting."

I'm still looking him over, and can't help but notice how even after wearing a helmet, his white hair is styled perfectly.

"It's the truth, Genevieve," he says.

The sound of my name breaks my focus on his aesthetics.

"You know who—" He laughs.

"What's so funny?" I raise my voice to be heard over his laughter.

He's really starting to annoy me.

"You!" He laughs again. "Because you're stupid. Of course I know you. Why would you assume I didn't?"

"Oh, I don't know. Maybe because I've never met you before," I hiss, my face flushing. "You know what? You're a real jerk. And you're acting like I'm an imbecile for not knowing what the hell is going on around here. I mean, sure, thanks for saving me. But if this is how you're going to treat me, then you and I have a real problem."

"Oh, hush." He groans. "Are you truly the girl that the future of Banewind depends upon?"

My heart drops into my stomach as I piece together what's going on.

"This...this is Banewind." I falter as my vision clouds, panic coursing through my body, and nausea rises into my throat.

"Yes." He's staring at me now, a smirk spreading across his lips. "Not the homecoming you were expecting, huh?"

"Where's Jensen!" I recall the last time I saw him in the cemetery. "What have you done to him?"

"I haven't done anything to him, Genevieve. He isn't here." The young man glares at me. "And by the way, that sounded accusatory."

"It was meant to be," I growl. "I want to go back home. *Now.*"

"All right, we obviously got off on the wrong foot." He steps forward and extends his hand toward me. "My name is Kingston Starmantle, and I'm a friend of the Saint Clair family."

I hesitate before grabbing his hand. "Genevieve DeWinter."

I wait for him to respond.

When he doesn't, I say, "So where are we exactly?"

"We are in the Voidlands." He lets go of my hand and motions around us. "And this, Genevieve, is the Court of Anguish."

I take in the surroundings, and see nothing but the abyss that lies below the land's edge. In the distance, on the courtyard's other side, is a towering black castle piercing the night's sky. Its structure dominates the earth in dark shadows.

"How did I get here?" I whisper.

"You were sent here through a portal. No, not by me," he says, before I can interject. "By a woman named Valkryn. She was at the cemetery with the Magician."

I remember the woman's voice shouting my name right before I disappeared.

"So how did you find me?"

"I didn't find you. I came through the portal with you." Kingston looks down at the ground, as if he's embarrassed. "I was keeping an eye on you at the cemetery as well. When I realized what Valkryn was doing...well, I couldn't let that happen, obviously."

"So you've been following me, too. But why?"

"I was doing it as a favor."

"A *favor*? A favor for who?"

"Just someone. Look, it doesn't matter, does it? I kept you safe, and that's what's important." He puts his helmet back on. "But now we have to get you home."

"Ah, and that's where I come in?"

The same voice from earlier echoes through the sky, but still there is no one else around us.

"Unfortunately, yes," Kingston says. "Do you mind showing yourself, Naxx?"

"But certainly."

The air nearby begins to stir. A figure appears in front of me, as if stepping out of another dimension. The form it takes resembles a human, but its body is nothing more than dark, swirling mist encased in a clear vessel. Its silver robe drapes down to the ground, barely touching the earth, giving the illusion that it's hovering.

"There we are." Its voice sounds distant, although it stands mere feet from me. "I apologize for any trepidation my appearance may have caused you, Lady Genevieve." Its robe's lavish sleeves brush against the ground as it bows to me. "I would have revealed myself sooner, but alas, the tension of battle does nothing but provide me constant angst."

"It's, um...it's okay." I try to be polite and make eye contact with it, but it has no distinguishable facial features.

"Oh! Why yes, of course, of course." The purple mist swirling inside the humanoid vessel flutters around. "Where are my manners, dear girl? You know nothing of my kind, do you!"

"I, uh, I don't. I'm sorry."

"Please. No apology necessary." It clears its throat—or at least, I think that's what it's doing. "My name is Naxxorius. But you, like so many others, may call me Naxx."

"Naxx here is an elemental," Kingston says. "He's the result of Formulist magic. An artifact, if you will. They call themselves the *Visidium*."

"Visidium?" I watch as Naxxorius crosses his arms. "So there are more of you?"

"Oh, heavens, yes." Naxxorius says. "Hundreds of us, actually. You see, we are created from the essence of each school of magic. For example, I am made from shadow. Some from fire. Others, ice. You understand, ah?"

"Sure. But how do you...well, *look* the way you do?"

"You mean, my casing?" Naxxorius motions to his body. "These are man-made, my dear. Silversong Glass, the strongest material you'll find in Banewind. When it was discovered that certain elements were...*alive*—for lack of a better word—the Formulists searched for a way to give us physical entities. After a period of manufacturing and prototypes, these elemental vessels were developed." He chortles. "Although I can reassure you, as constructed as we may appear, each one of us is unique, with our own spirit and personality. We are very much our own working conscience."

"I see." *I mean, really. What else is there to say?*

"So," Naxxorius turns his head towards Kingston, "I suppose this is the part where you pay me our agreed stipend?"

Kingston scoffs. "This is why I hate doing work with elementals like you." He reaches into his armor below his neck, and pulls out a small brown sack. "Here's your gold."

Naxxorius extends his long, spider-like fingers until

they are grasped around the bag.

"The foolish man's way is the poor man's brother, ah?" The elemental weighs the bag in his hand before stowing it in his robes. "Just remember all the good this is doing for Lady Genevieve."

"Excuse me?" I look to Kingston.

"The portal you came in on routed you to the access point back in the gorge. You remember? It was that black platform you were on."

"Okay." I'm still not sure what he's telling me.

"Well, I deactivated it once we were here so that nobody could follow us through. Which, unfortunately, means that we have to find another point to take you back home."

"And where is that?" I say, afraid of his reply.

"Inside the Void Keep." He laughs, gesturing to the black castle. "And trust me, that is the last place you want to be right now."

I fail to see the humor in this situation.

"However," he points his thumb at Naxxorius, "my frugal friend is lucky enough to have the ability to create access points from anywhere he wants."

"And all for one flat-rate fee," Naxxorius says. "You are just fortunate that I spend my idle time wandering around these decrepit lands."

"Yeah. That, and everyone was dealing with the summoned Shadow Dredger."

I can tell Kingston is smirking behind the helmet.

"I didn't know how I was going to get Naxxorius from the Court of Anguish without drawing attention. But luckily, fate had a way of figuring that out for us."

"Why would anyone summon that thing?" I shudder as I glance back at its ashen remains.

"Because the Court of Anguish is the training ground for the Dark Lady's army." Before I can ask another question, he holds up his hand. "I'm sorry, Genevieve. But now isn't the time for this. You really have to go before she discovers you're here." Kingston nods to Naxxorius. "The access point, please."

Naxxorius waves his hand over the ground, and a small mound of earth rises.

"Step onto it, Genevieve." Kingston pulls out an octahedral-shaped crystal and holds it in front of him, grasping it between his hands.

I place my foot onto the darkened earth.

"Are you ready?" Kingston says.

"What is that?" I nod to the object.

"A portal key. I'm using it to send you home."

"Am I going to see you again?"

The butterflies in my stomach have emerged, and are now zooming around in full frenzy.

"For your sake, Genevieve, I hope not."

"Wait. What does that mean?"

"Good luck. Tell Jensen I said hello."

"What does that mean!"

The world around me explodes into white as I feel myself disappear.

13

BRUISES

WHEN I WAS IN PHYSICS LAST YEAR, our teacher loved to show us videos on pilots training to withstand the extreme gravitational force exerted on them while traveling into space. I remember wondering what it must have felt like to have nine Gs crushing down on your body, sometimes forcing you into a state of unconsciousness.

Although I was content with never finding out the answer to that question, I'm pretty sure I just did.

My back slams onto the ground, knocking out the little air I had left inside my lungs. Every bone jars against my skin, and I hear every sound within me ring from one ear to the other. I swear I've just broken into a million pieces.

My hands are at my side, and I realize they're pressed against something soft. I turn my head and see a maroon oriental rug decorating the floor I'm on. There are no lights except the sliver of moonlight peaking in from behind the nearby window curtains. Amidst the ringing in my ears, I hear a ticking clock. And then footsteps. They're coming fast. And I can do nothing but lie here.

I watch as a door opens, allowing the light from the

hallway to seep into the room. The figure standing there is obscured by shadow, but within seconds I'm squinting at the now illuminated ceiling.

"Oh, Genevieve!" Sadie's words dance across the air in trembling sounds. "Yeah, it's her, Jensen. She's...yes, I will. Okay, see you soon." I hear her cell phone click off. "We thought you were dead!"

"Yeah, I wasn't sure there for a while, either."

I don't think she appreciates my humor.

"Are you hurt?" She rushes over and kneels next to me. "Jensen is on his way back. He's been out looking for you all over town."

"Sadie," I whisper, and take a deep breath. "I'll be okay in a minute. I just had the wind knocked out of me." I reach out toward her. "Help me up. Thanks."

"Careful." Her voice doesn't seem as frightened as before. "How are you feeling?"

"My head feels like it's been used in a soccer game. But besides that, I've felt..." I remember the cemetery. "Jensen! Wait, he's okay? He's not hurt?"

"He's fine, Genevieve." Sadie helps me to my feet, then pulls out the leather chair from the nearby desk and guides me into it. "Once he got out of the cemetery, he came right back here to look for you. When he found out you weren't here...well, we were just praying you had escaped to somewhere." She looks around the room. "Although, I don't think we were expecting you to come through a portal."

I hear the front door slam shut. My heart begins to race as I hear the footsteps bounding up the stairs.

"Genevieve!" Jensen envelops me in a warm embrace. The grogginess in my head clears, and my heart leaps into my throat, pulsing the blood throughout my body.

He pulls away and rests his head against mine, breathing his warmth into my ear.

"I was so afraid, Genevieve," he whispers. "I thought I had lost you. I thought I had failed you." He pulls back and looks at me. The normal light in his brown eyes is obscured by concern. "I am so, so sorry."

"Genevieve, what happened after you were separated from Jensen?" Sadie re-ties her periwinkle bathrobe before settling onto the brown ottoman next to me.

"It...it all happened so fast." I close my eyes as I replay the events in my mind. "I started to run back to look for him, but before I made it far, I was...gone. Gone from here, anyway. I had been transported to Banewind."

The color drains from Sadie's face.

"You were there?" Jensen places his hand into mine.

I nod. "I was in the Court of Anguish."

"Heavens to Lura!" Sadie rests her trembling fingers against her lips. "What happened next?"

"Some creature was attacking. I don't remember the name. Shadow something..."

"Dredger," Sadie says.

I can't tell now if hers or Jensen's face is whiter.

"Yeah, that's it. Anyway, Kingston defeated it, and then he sent me back here." I look at Jensen." He said he knew you."

His face darkens with anger. "Kingston?" he hisses, glaring at Sadie. "Did you hear what she said?"

"He followed me through the portal, from the cemetery."

I have a sneaking suspicion he's not going to like hearing that.

When his face turns five shades of a darker scarlet, he's confirmed it for me.

"I'm calling Casius," Jensen growls, letting go of my hand, and stomps out of the room.

Sadie acknowledges my confusion with a deep sigh.

"Casius is Jensen's older brother," she says. "They don't always see eye to eye."

"And Kingston?"

Sadie shakes her head. "Like I said, they don't always see things the same way." She waits a moment. "Genevieve, did Kingston tell you anything else?"

"Well, he told me I was sent through the portal by some woman. Valkryn, I think her name was? And that she's trying to kill me, too. So...yeah."

Sadie presses her fingertips against her forehead and rubs hard.

"Oh, we are not ready for this. We just aren't." She stares blankly at me and sighs. "Genevieve, I need to go discuss a few things with Jensen. Why don't you get some rest? I'll take you into Jensen's room to lie down."

As if on cue, a wave of exhaustion rolls over me.

"That sounds great." I look down at my dirty, ripped clothes. "Um, actually, do you mind if I take a shower first and borrow one of your nightgowns? I'd rather not look like I just crawled out from a cemetery."

No pun intended.

Trust me. I'm too tired for that.

I don't know how long I've been lying in bed when I hear the door creak open.

"Hey," I whisper into the darkness. "How are you?"

"Shh. Go back to sleep, Genevieve. It's late." Jensen

shuts the door behind him. "I was trying not to wake you."

"I haven't been asleep." I sit up and place a pillow behind me, against the headboard. "There's just too much on my mind."

He sighs. "Yeah, I can imagine." He points his hand at the fireplace in the corner of the room, and it jumps to life, its flames illuminating the darkness.

I watch as he pulls off his shirt and places it into the wardrobe. His stomach muscles tighten as he bends over to remove his pants, and changes into a pair of workout shorts. He is a vision of perfection.

"What did you and Sadie talk about?" I'm still focused on his physique.

His back muscles ripple across his skin like ocean waves as he pulls closed the wardrobe doors.

"Just the situation," he replies. "If I'm being honest, we're concerned that the two of us aren't going to be enough to protect you from what's to come. That both the Magician and Valkryn are already here in town is something we didn't foresee happening. It's just not good." He looks over at me. "Is it all right if I get into bed with you?"

"Yeah, of course."

My heartbeat fills the bedroom as he climbs into bed next to me. I feel the heat radiating from his torso.

"So who are they?" I try not to stare too much at his chiseled stomach. "The Magician and Valkryn?"

"They're Voidweavers that work with the Dark Lady. Commanders, no less. The Magician is her chief engineer. He's in charge of creating all sorts of terrible devices that they've used to terrorize Banewind. And Valkryn is a shadow mage that helps command the Void Knights." He sighs. "They're very bad people."

"Yeah, I got that." I shudder as I remember the

jarring sensation of being pulled through the portal. "And... what happened to Scythe?"

"I don't know." His body tenses. "I left him in the mausoleum."

"Do you think that he's the one who told the Magician where to find me?"

The words are hard to speak. I had trusted Scythe, and was sure he was trying to help.

"Genevieve, after tonight, you cannot honestly believe he's looking out for your best interests? They nearly got you!"

"Okay, yes, it did *appear* that Scythe was still working with the Magician. But I'm not so sure that was the case. I mean, Scythe seemed just as upset as you were. And what about the note? And the necklace?"

"Genevieve." Jensen exhales and closes his eyes. "I don't know. But based on his actions... I'm just so sorry. For all of this. It seems like everything I've done up to this point has been wrong. And I don't know what to do to make it right. I feel lost. The only good coming out of tonight is now that the Magician and Valkryn have actually made a move, it provides us a stronger case to try to rally the Council's support. Sadie is going to speak with them tomorrow evening."

I sit quietly on the bed.

"Genevieve? Say something."

"I really don't know what to say. We're doing the best we can. No one's at fault for what's going on. Not you, not Sadie." I reach over and rub his arm, his skin hot beneath my touch. "It'll all work out, Jensen. I promise."

I move myself closer to his body and trace my fingertips over his shoulder, then run them down his collarbone. He closes his eyes as I rest my head against his.

My breath is quickening, and my heart leaps into my throat.

He nuzzles his face into my neck, and I feel his warm breath cascade across my skin. The familiarity of my senses heightening takes over as every nerve fiber in my body jolts to life. I close my eyes as I feel his lips just barely brush against my neck, toying with my skin between his teeth. The air I exhale is shallow and broken, painted with bursts of pleasure.

"Kiss me," I whisper, hearing my words convulse as they pass between my lips.

I slide my hands to his chest and grasp, feeling his muscles quaver beneath my touch.

"Kiss me, Jensen."

He presses his lips against mine, and I kiss him back, panting as I slide my hand up his chest and cradle his chin within my palm. His hand is against my face, and he grasps at my hair, pulling it towards him, and me along with it. The world has shattered and slipped away.

I pull back and smile at him.

"What?" A grin spreads across his face.

"Nothing." I giggle. "Just thinking how that makes up for everything I've gone through tonight."

I rest my head on his chest as he rubs my hair, and within moments I'm fast asleep.

CRASH!

My eyes snap open at the deafening sound. I don't know how long I've been asleep, but Jensen is no longer beside me.

CRACK!

"Stop it! Stop!" Sadie screams, from downstairs. "Jensen, no!"

Oh, God. Jensen!

I throw the covers from my body and leap out of bed. As I rush from the room, I hear shouts echoing through the hallway, becoming louder as I near the stairway.

"Jensen, please!" Sadie is standing at the far end of the living room, surrounded by fallen bookshelves and scattered papers.

The couch is flipped upside down, and the glass coffee table is shattered into pieces. The nearby floor is scorched black, with dark wisps of smoke winding into the air.

And in the center of it all are Jensen and Scythe. Jensen is sitting on top of Scythe's chest, pinning him down. I watch in horror as Jensen pounds his fists into Scythe's face, spattering blood across the white marble floor.

My stomach ties into knots as I rush down the staircase.

"Jensen! What are you doing? Stop it!" My screams are barely audible over the fighting. "Jensen, stop!"

I grab his fist as he pulls it back, breaking his focus on Scythe. He spins around and glares at me with dark, irate eyes, his nostrils flaring, and veins protruding from his neck.

"Jensen, please stop." I try to hold back my fear.

Scythe is still under Jensen, barely moving. His face is coated with bright, oozing blood.

"Get back upstairs, Genevieve," Jensen growls. "This isn't your fight."

"And it isn't yours, either." I point to Scythe. "Look what you've done to him. He can hardly move. You've won, Jensen, okay? Please, just stop."

He hesitates before removing himself from Scythe.

"Thank you," I whisper.

He wipes his bloodied knuckles on his shorts, but says nothing.

"Uhhh," Scythe moans, gingerly lifting his head.

His left eye is swollen shut, and his black hair is stuck to his forehead with blood. He takes his time getting to his feet.

"If you were trying to hurt me..." He spits blood out onto the floor, "...you're going to have to do better than that, fire mage."

I grab Jensen's shoulder, feeling it tense beneath my hand.

"No, Jensen, please," I say, into his ear.

Scythe looks at my nightgown and frowns.

"I came by to make sure you were doing okay," he says. "For what it's worth, I didn't know the Magician was going to be there." He gestures to Sadie. "Please just give me a chance to—"

"Get out." Jensen points to the front doors.

A cold silence hangs in the air.

Scythe laughs. "Fine. Whatever." He wipes his bloodied mouth on the back of his hand as he limps toward the doors. "If you don't want to hear what I have to say, I'll go."

He disappears into the starlit dawn.

"I'm sorry." Jensen slouches onto the nearby chaise longue. "I opened the door and saw him standing there... and I don't know what happened. I lost my temper. I wasn't thinking." He stares at his bloodied knuckles. "I don't...I..."

"It's okay." Sadie rubs his back. "Why don't you go get cleaned up? I'll take Genevieve back home now."

Jensen slowly stands from the longue, and pauses as he walks by me.

"I'm sorry."

I reach out and squeeze his hand. "It's okay. I understand. I'll see you at school."

He heads back upstairs.

"Your clothes are in the dryer," Sadie says. "Let me go grab them for you. I'll be back in a moment."

I stand there alone in the empty room, my feet cold against the marble floor.

The grandfather clock chimes five times.

14

PROGRESS

"Ah, there she is." The Magician grunts without breaking his focus from the project in front of him. "Are you finally convinced that the girl is no longer in Banewind, then?"

He continues kneeling on the floor as he tightens the bolts into a metal disc. Several colorful wires protrude from its side, jutting out from a silver box with electronic numbers dancing across its screen.

"Done wasting your time?" he says.

"I find it no more a waste of time than you tinkering with your toys," Valkryn replies.

Her green boots click against the church's faded marble as she moves toward the Magician.

She pauses at the pew besides him. "But of course, I don't expect you to agree."

"I'm curious, Valkryn," he sets down his wrench and stands, "as to what better plan you can propose. Because the way I see it, we are out of options."

Valkryn pulls her purple shawl tighter around her shoulders as she sits in the pew. Her silver hair falls in wavy curls over her face, obscuring most of her features. Her lime-green lips part into a wicked smile.

"Do you suppose, Blaine, that the reason our options are so limited at this point is because of you?"

"You're the one who thought Scythe could be a valuable asset," he snarls. "I will not take responsibility for the orphan's foolishness." He grabs a screwdriver from the nearby toolbox. "Do not blame me for his incompetence."

"Not any more incompetent than you, I would say."

The Magician slams the screwdriver into the back of the wooden pew, mere inches from Valkryn's neck.

"You are testing my patience, shadow mage," he hisses.

Her emerald eyes burn bright with fervor.

"The hostility you feel towards me," she rises from the pew and walks over to the church's vestibule doors, "just needs to be redirected to the task at hand." She picks up the Magician's crumpled orange hat on a nearby counter, tracing the brim through her slender, pale fingers. "It says something that the Dark Lady chose both of us to find the girl for her, no?"

"*Bah*," the Magician scoffs, flicking his hand at Valkryn. "She only picked us because nobody else believes her delusions about this paladin nonsense." He gets back onto the ground and begins to thread another wire into the metal plate. "And I'm beginning to believe we were dumb enough to go along with it as well."

"Is that so?" Valkryn glances at him. "Then why continue helping?"

"Don't be daft, Val. Would you rather us die if we said no?" He clears his throat and runs his hand through his slick black hair. "And what? I suppose you're going to tell me your motives are simply altruistic in helping?"

Valkryn smirks. "We both know altruism doesn't

exist." She throws his hat to him. "Everything is done with ulterior motives in mind."

"Perhaps the smartest thing I've heard you say." The Magician knocks his fist against the metal plate. "Almost ready."

Valkryn's black amethyst suit tightens as she folds her arms across her chest, cocking her head as she stares at the silver contraption fixed into the floor.

"You're becoming skilled at makeshift portals, aren't you?" She taps her boot against the metal. "Surprising, given your other recent experiment failures."

"I'm offended by your lack of trust."

Valkryn rolls her eyes. "Oh, don't be so sensitive. I just want to make sure we'll get the girl this time."

"The portal leads right into my laboratory. When the girl comes through, I'll be waiting there for her."

"And Saint Clair? I'm assuming he'll be accompanying her."

The Magician laughs. "*Tsk, tsk*, Val. I'm disappointed you aren't up to date on things." His black beady eyes widen with excitement. "Saint Clair will not be a problem. I have been assured he will be called away, leaving Miss DeWinter vulnerable to our actions. It is Scythe that will be with her. I am sure of it."

Valkryn's eyebrows arch in surprise. "I thought we established that he is no longer cooperating with us?"

"The boy is no longer considered an ally to us, that is correct." The Magician looks around the church. "However, he is the closest thing we have that Miss DeWinter trusts. And so we still must use him as a pawn."

"That seems like an awfully big risk to take."

He shakes his head as he closes his eyes.

"If I can stop one heart from breaking,
I shall not live in vain.
If I can ease one life the aching,
Or cool one pain,
Or help one fainting robin
Unto his nest again,
I shall not live in vain."

"Oh, finally putting your literature studies to good use?" Valkryn says. "Maybe your time at the Academy was well-spent, after all."

"Emily Dickinson." The Magician strokes his black goatee. "Depressing woman, but hell of a good understanding of life."

"What's your point?"

"My point, Valkryn, is that Scythe has feelings for Miss DeWinter. That much is obvious. And he will do what he can to help her. Even if it means unknowingly putting her into harm's way."

"Go on."

The Magician chuckles. "He will bring the girl to the church himself. And when he does, that will be the end of them both."

"But how do you know this will work?" Valkryn's voice echoes amidst the high-set ceilings. "They will suspect a trap."

"Because just as Scythe wants to protect Genevieve," he glares at Valkryn, "so, too, does she want to protect her younger brother."

A shrill sound shatters the church's silence.

"Well, well." Valkryn reaches down into the black pochette hanging over her shoulder. "Let's hope your confidence comes across as strong to the Dark Lady."

She pulls out a glowing orb and releases it from her hand. It floats amidst a swirl of black fog. The sound amplifies into a howling screech as purple light projects from the levitating object. The Dark Lady's head merges into focus, shrouded by the black fog.

"Valkryn," she says, her voice a haunting echo. "Are you with Blaine?"

"I'm here, Dark Lady." The Magician walks around to stand next to Valkryn.

The Dark Lady's eyes glow deep amethyst beneath her bird skull, piercing at her commanders.

"What is transpiring?" she says.

"The portal is about ready to go," the Magician replies. "I just need a little more time to make sure it's functioning properly."

"I will not tolerate further failure, Blaine. That the girl was in Banewind once already and avoided detection is...unacceptable. Do we know yet how she escaped?"

The Magician eyes Valkryn.

"We're not sure who helped her, no," she says. "But rest assured, she will not evade us again."

"Every moment she spends with her allies is a risk to our own endeavors. Am I to assume you need not be reminded of this?"

"Absolutely," the Magician says. "We understand."

"If I am to have any hope of returning to my former power, she *must* be acquired as soon as possible." The Dark Lady scowls. "Dorndrick Wolfshire and the Abolishment have already started to re-emerge. It is only a matter of time before they regain their full strength. We cannot allow that."

"Yes, that...that would be problematic." The Magician strokes his black goatee. "Have you made grounds on where they're organizing? If we could infiltrate their headquarters—"

"I did not ask for your input. Your words are unappreciated."

"My apologies."

"Dorndrick Wolfshire knows that Addisyn DeWinter is not dead," the Dark Lady says. "He has learned what happened, and he knows about the Binding Spell."

"What?" Valkryn says. "How?"

"Mengurion Maldridge. Even locked away in a cell, the frail old fool continues to cause me grief. I am no longer sure of the utility of keeping him alive."

"That's unfortunate." Valkryn frowns. "But understandable."

"Blaine, I need to know where we stand on Project Corlynnia," the Dark Lady says. "How is it coming along?"

"It, ah…it has been halted momentarily while I have pursued the girl. But also almost complete."

"So many unfinished things," the Dark Lady hisses. "You disappoint me."

"I can assure you, the prototypes are almost ready for testing. Just a few more tweaks. I'll get to work on them the moment I'm back in Banewind…with the girl, of course. Is there…anything else we can do for you at the moment?"

"Get the girl," she growls. "And we will go on from there."

Her face fades away as the orb shrieks out once more, blinding the church in a purple flash, before falling to the floor with a *thud!*

The Magician and Valkryn stand alone in silence.

15

UNCLE

I REMAIN QUIET IN THE CAR WITH SADIE for most of the trip back to my house, replaying the night's events in my head. When she stops the car in our driveway, I don't get out.

"Genevieve? What are you thinking about?"

"Did you know?" I twist my mother's necklace between my fingers.

"Did I know—"

"Did you know that my mother's body wasn't in her casket?" I choke on the words, holding back tears once again.

Sadie sits in silence.

"Yes," she finally replies. "I did. And if I would have known that you were planning to go to the cemetery, I would have told you that. But I was not keeping anything from you about your mother still being alive. From what I know, she perished in her final battle with the Void King. Just because they couldn't find her body..." She shakes her head. "But finding her necklace? She wore that until the very end. She never took it off. I don't know where it could have come from. And now, if you were to ask me if she's alive or dead?" She sighs. "I have no answer for you."

I ponder her words before opening the door and stepping out into the morning's crisp air. I walk into the house without looking back, and arrive before my family is even awake. I sit at the kitchen counter with a bowl of cereal, pushing around its contents with a spoon, lost in my thoughts.

"Good morning, Jeannie." Dad yawns as he stumbles into the kitchen in his fuzzy blue slippers.

I had been hoping to be off to school before he ran into me.

"You're up nice and early today." He pulls out his mug with WORLD'S #1 DAD stamped on the front, which Danny bought for him the Christmas before last.

I pick up a spoonful of cereal and let it drop back into the bowl.

"What's wrong? Rough night?"

"Yeah. I've had better."

"Up late with homework?"

Genevieve, don't say it. Now is not the time. Don't say it.

"Actually, I went out to the cemetery. And you'll probably get a call from them later, because I'm pretty sure the mausoleum was destroyed. But it doesn't really matter, does it? It's not like my mother is even in there."

"What?" He flinches. "Jeannie, what do you—"

"I know, Dad." I look him in the eyes. "I know about the Formulists."

The color drains from his face as he falters, catching himself on the counter.

"You...you what?"

"I know the truth." I raise my voice. "I know about Banewind. I know about the Void King. I know that Mom was a paladin. I know."

"Jeannie, but...I...how—"

"Sadie Hawthorne and Jensen Saint Clair. Do those names sound familiar to you? I'm sure they do." My face is hot. "They're back in Parma. Trying to protect me. Because, turns out, they think I might be a paladin as well."

He walks over to the kitchen table and pulls out a chair, avoiding my gaze.

"The Voidweavers are back." I pull off my necklace and hand it to him. "Recognize this?"

He slowly reaches out and takes the necklace in his hand, examining its pendant.

"Yeah, that's right." My voice cracks. "That's Mom's, isn't it?"

He sits in silence for a moment longer, before taking off his glasses and setting them on the kitchen table.

"Your uncle gave this to her," he whispers, caressing the sapphires. "Never met the guy. I only knew how much it meant to her. She never took it off. Even until..." His voice breaks. "She never took it off." He looks up at me, his eyes misty. "Oh, Jeannie. I am so, so sorry."

"Why didn't you ever tell me? I understand when I was younger. But even now? I'm an adult, Dad, and yet you still didn't think I should know the truth about my mother's life?"

"Jeannie, please." He rubs his moustache. "You have to understand that I was trying to protect you. There was no need for you to know. Banewind died with her."

"No, it didn't. No, Dad, it didn't. An entire world doesn't just *die*. Not unless you make yourself think it did."

"I didn't know much about it, Jeannie." He takes a deep breath. "I only knew that it existed, and that your mother was part of something I couldn't possibly comprehend. You have to understand, there was no malintent. She didn't want you to know, either!"

"I don't believe that." I shake my head. "No. She knew that one day I could be pulled into this. I'm sure she did. And now she might not even be..."

I see the pain in my father's eyes, and the realization hits me that there is no blame to put on him. That he was just as blind to everything going on as I was.

"She's not even here to tell me herself."

I can't bring myself to say she might still be alive, especially when I don't even know if that's true. I don't need to hurt my father any more than I already have.

"What's going on?" Danny enters the kitchen, wearing a tank top and boxers. "I thought I heard yelling."

"Nothing, Daniel. Go back to bed," Dad says.

"Sorry, squirt." I look over at my father. "We were just talking about how Monday is Labor Day, and we forgot to plan for a party."

"Oh, well. You've woken me up, so thanks for that. I'm gonna go get ready for school." He turns around and heads back upstairs.

I walk over to my father, and he stands from his chair. I wrap my arms around him and hug him tight.

"I'm sorry," I whisper. "I shouldn't have told you like that."

"It's okay, Jeannie. You don't need to apologize." He pulls away from me, but continues to hold my shoulders. "Now, are you going to tell me what you know?"

I glance at the clock. "I have to go to school. But we can talk about this later, all right?"

He frowns. "Are you in danger?"

"Not at the moment." I try to smile, realizing the possible repercussions I've created by telling him about this. "And I know that's a lot to drop on you first thing in the morning, but I promise I'm okay. Can you trust me on that?"

"I trust you." He hands me my mother's necklace. "But we will sit down and talk about this eventually, all right?"

I kiss him on the cheek before heading out of the house.

This is already turning into a long day.

I'm surprised to see Katie standing next to my locker as I turn down the hallway. Wasn't expecting anyone else to be here yet this early.

As I make eye contact with her, I see that her face is as white as a sheet. Her body is trembling, and her eyes are on the brim of tears behind her glasses. She's clutching the Formulist book to her chest.

"Katie? What's wrong?"

"This." She gestures her chin at the book.

"I...you mean, the book?" I glance at the faded binding. "Why? What's wrong with it?"

"What's going on over here?"

I hear Jensen's voice and turn around and see him just inches from me. His eyebrows are furrowed as he stares at Katie.

"I don't know yet," I reply.

Jensen is staring at the Formulist book.

He frowns at me. "Oh, no, Genevieve. Did you..."

"I had to tell her. She's my best friend. Katie, what's going on?" I say, in a gentle voice. "Did you find something out?"

"Y-yes." She nods.

I can tell Jensen is as confused as I am.

"Katie, what are you talking about?" he says. "What did you find?"

She opens the book and pulls out a slim flash drive from in between the pages.

"I found it hidden in a rip of the back cover, last night." She gasps, her words broken. "I thought it was just more information on the book. I called you a dozen times, but you didn't answer, Genevieve."

"Katie, I am so, so sorry. I didn't even know you called. Last night I..." *Oh, crap! My phone.* "Damnit!"

I plunge my hands into my pockets before taking off my backpack and scouring through it.

"What's wrong?"

"My phone, Jensen. I think I lost it." I continue to throw papers around the floor. "I haven't seen it since Banewind."

"You were in Banewind?" Katie squeaks, her voice plagued with fear.

"Yeah. I have a lot to catch you up on. But Katie, you have to tell us what you found."

She holds the flash drive out for us. "It's a message from Genevieve's uncle. Right before he was murdered."

We are now in Sadie's classroom. After Katie decided to drop that bombshell on us, Jensen suggested we continue the conversation in Sadie's presence. Luckily, we still had some time before school started.

"I told you I knew your uncle, yes," Sadie is at her computer, inserting the flash drive as the projection screen lowers in front of the chalkboard. "But your mother's family was complicated. After she defeated the Void King, we never heard from him again."

"I didn't know the flash drive was in there." Jensen picks up the book from the desk. "And I still don't understand how it got there."

"Is the book yours?" I watch as he flips through the pages.

Jensen frowns. "It's not mine, no. It's my father's. But he didn't give it to me. I just took it from his library. So I doubt he had anything to do with it."

The computer beeps, and the flash drive's folder pops up. Its contents consist of a video file and a single document titled *F*.

"The document is...weird," Katie says. "I checked that out first."

Sadie opens the file, and I see its contents displayed on the projection screen.

$$Map\ (I)$$
$$A = 1 \times 4 + F = 1 \times 3$$
$$4$$
$$5$$
$$9$$
$$14$$
$$17$$
$$6$$
$$23$$
$$5\ 2\ 6 - 7\ 3\ 4\ 1$$
$$Text\ (II)$$
$$X = 0.\ 1,\ 2,\ 3,\ 4(x),\ 5(x),\ ...$$
$$B + Y = FIRST$$
$$1 + 2 = 3$$

"Uh..." I stare at the screen, mouth open. "Does anyone know what this is?"

"Some kind of code." Katie sighs. "But I haven't had time to work on deciphering it."

"All right. Well, why don't we put that on hold for now." Sadie closes the document. "Are you ready?" She clicks on the video.

"I'm sorry. I can't watch it again." Katie stands and heads for the door, but stops as she grabs the handle. "I'll be back for class." She slips out into the hallway.

I glance at the clock. "Do we have time to watch it?"

"We should." Sadie clicks on the computer.

The projection screen goes dark. And then there is a man staring back at me. I hold my breath, waiting for him to speak.

"Hello, Genevieve," he whispers. "I apologize for this hasty recording. But given my current circumstances, I would say it's pretty damn impressive that I'm pulling it off."

A siren blares in the background, nearly drowning out his quiet voice. He is sitting in some sort of a lab, surrounded by computer monitors and other high-tech machines.

"Now Genevieve, it is unfortunate that this is the way I must introduce myself to you. But we don't have a lot of time."

He takes off his glasses and places them on top of his blond hair. His forehead is caked with blood, and his cheeks bruised and beaten. But his blue eyes are identical to my mother's, and before he even says the words, I know he is related to me.

"In a few minutes, I will be dead, and I will never know if this recording made it safely to you." He frowns.

"There are very few people left to trust in this world. But even amidst all the hatred, the anger, the fighting, I believe there are some who have not yet lost their way. Sadly, it is too late for me.

"Genevieve, my name is Felyx Crimsley, and I am your uncle. I'm sure this news comes as a...surprise to you. But you must understand, there are very good reasons that your mother never told you about me. I don't have time to pursue this matter further, but I am confident that one day all will be revealed. What you need to understand, Genevieve, is that everything you think you've learned, everything you think you know right now, is a lie. I am well-aware that by the time this reaches you, you will have already become acquainted with several Formulists. They, too, have been misinformed."

"What is he talking about?" Jensen's body is rigid behind the desk. "Sadie, what is he talking about?"

"They believe they are protecting you," Felyx says. "They believe you are what the Dark Lady wants. And they are wrong. Everyone is wrong. What they don't know is—"

Static screeches out of the speakers as the recording cuts out, splitting the image in several pieces. I jump in my seat as a *bang!* bursts from the speakers.

The recording comes back into focus, and I see Felyx snap his head around toward the steel doors at the back of the lab.

He returns to the camera. "That was quicker than I thought."

The pounding on the lab door grows louder.

"Genevieve, you must find Isaac Banewind, or my death is for nothing."

In the background, I see the hinges fall off the steel doors, the indentations growing with every furious pound.

"Don't be afraid, Genevieve."

Bang! Bang! Bang!

"Goodbye."

The lab's back wall splits in two with a mighty explosion, launching pieces of the metal door in all directions. Sparks hiss, and smoke swirls around the room as the debris collides with various machines. Felyx remains in the center, his white lab coat fluttering in the stirred air.

The smoke clears, bringing with it the emergence of a towering man clad in black armor, and casting a looming shadow across the room. His hands are folded at his chest, and the helmet he wears is designed in the shape of a bull's head.

A woman follows. As she moves through the fallen rubble, toward the two men, her steps are smooth and graceful, as if she is gliding across the ground. Her black dress snugs her body, revealing a slender yet powerful-looking physique. And the matching gloves she wears rise to her elbows, a stark contrast against her snow-white skin. On each shoulder rests an armored plate, embedded with amethyst crystals that reflect in the lab's flickering lights. And a dark purple cape ripples down her back, hitting the floor like a glass of spilt wine.

But her face is hidden beneath some sort of skull adornment. It is elongated, with large, round eye sockets and two ridges at the nostrils which come together at the tip of a thick, piercing beak projecting out in front of her. The only visible feature is her thin, red lips curled into a hideous scowl.

"Felyx." Her voice is hollow, sounding like a distant echo.

She raises her hand and places it on the side of his face.

"What a disappointment you are to me. So much potential. So much possibility. And yet here we are."

"I am sorry to disappoint you, *Dark Lady*," Felyx hisses.

She turns to her soldier and nods.

He grabs Felyx by the neck with one hand, lifting him into the air. His other hand glows a searing orange, the flames crackling like mocking laughter, taunting Genevieve's uncle. The soldier thrusts his arm forward, and the fireball catches on Felyx's lab coat. His screams fill the room as the soldier releases him, where he remains floating in the air.

Flames spread across Felyx's body, engulfing him in a bright immolation. The screen flashes, and Felyx's agonizing howls cease. A charred, unrecognizable figure hangs in the air, the body black like a mummified corpse. The Dark Lady reaches out her gloved hand and touches Felyx, who disintegrates into a pile of ash.

"Burn it all, Vin'jork." The Dark Lady glides back towards the entrance. "There's nothing here but waste."

Vin'jork follows behind her, but turns back to the lab once she is out of the room. He looks around, his gaze briefly making contact with the camera. His hands glow bright red, and he thrusts them forward, casting a fireball that comes barreling towards us. There is a *whoosh!*, a *crash!*, and then nothing but static on the screen.

I feel my stomach gurgling, starting to push into my throat.

"I think I'm going to—"

I'm over at the trash next to Sadie's desk, spewing the contents from today's breakfast into the basket. I heave several more times, coughing with such force that I can't catch my breath. The tears sting my eyes, blurring my vision.

I feel a hand placed onto my back.

"It's all right," Jensen whispers, rubbing between my shoulder blades. "Shh. It's okay. Take a deep breath. In and out. That's it."

I kneel onto the floor, my hands trembling at my sides. I gain control of my breathing before opening my eyes. The screen still hums with static.

"What the hell just happened?" I whisper.

Sadie offers me the tissue box from her desk.

"I...I don't know." Her words tremble.

"Who is Isaac Banewind?" I say.

Sadie continues to shake her head. "It just doesn't make sense."

"Jensen?" I look to him. "Who is Isaac?"

He frowns. "Isaac Banewind was the son of the Royal Formulists. He was the prince of Banewind."

"Was?"

Jensen sighs. "He's dead now, Genevieve. Like I told you before, he and the entire Banewind family were murdered by the Void King."

"Then why would Felyx say we have to find him?" I start thinking of my mother's empty casket. "Could he still be alive?"

"It..." Jensen says. "It seems very, very unlikely."

"But not impossible?"

Jensen shrugs. "I don't know." He looks at Sadie. "Should you bring this up to the Council tonight?"

She bites her nails.

"Sadie?"

"What?"

"The Council. Are you going to bring this up when you meet with them?"

"No. I don't think we know who to even trust right now."

"Then what do we do?" I say.

"What about your father?" Sadie looks at Jensen.

His face turns ghostly white. "Absolutely not. We can handle this without getting the rest of the Saint Clairs involved."

"I'm not so sure we can anymore. It may be best if—"

"No, Sadie. We aren't jeopardizing his career. It's out of the question."

"Jensen, I vividly remember your father saying that—"

"Yes, I remember that, too. But you know, right now he's on thin ice with the Council. We don't need to make things worse."

The five-minute warning bell echoes over the PA.

"I'm going to run to the restroom to freshen up before class." I break the awkward silence that hangs between Sadie and Jensen. "Is that okay?"

"Yes, of course it is." Sadie pulls the flash drive out of the computer. "Go ahead and leave the door propped open when you leave. We're going to have to start getting through this day, sooner or later."

I don't even know what happened during my morning classes. I can't tell you one thing I learned. I feel like an empty shell, walking from room to room, replaying the recording in my mind. I try to push the graphic images out of my head, but that only seems to make things worse.

When fifth period rolls around, I find Katie standing outside the cafeteria. She leans against the wall, much too rigid for her usual happy-go-lucky self. Her eyes seem dark and distant, and the corners of her mouth are pulled into a frown.

She holds the Formulist book against her chest.

"I told Jensen we'd meet him in the library," I say. "You want to get lunch first?"

"Not hungry. Come on."

Truth be told, I guess I'm not too hungry, either.

We find Jensen and go to a table tucked away in the back corner of the library. I catch Katie up on what happened while I was in Banewind.

"So who's this Kingston?" she says to Jensen. "It sounds like he's friends with your family?"

"My brother's friend, more so. But Kingston is a Void Knight, and he's with the Voidweavers. So you can understand my trepidation in trusting him."

"He's a Voidweaver?" I say. "But he helped me escape?"

Jensen shrugs. "He claims he's on our side. But I don't trust him."

"Well, regardless, he saved my life. So that says something," I add.

"And this Naxxorius? You said he's a Visidium?" Katie flips open the Formulist book to a page she had marked.

I see a sketch on the page that looks exactly like the creature I met.

"I read about them," Katie says. "Yeah. Like you said, they're elementals created from centuries of Formulist magic. They have their own society, too."

"That's correct," Jensen says. "Their city is called Axraxus. It's also in the Wastelands, near the Jintüroo."

He looks at me. "As Genevieve saw firsthand, they are a selfish group of creatures who function on a quid pro quo philosophy. They've remained neutral in most of their transgressions throughout Banewind's history, only doing things if it's in their own best interest."

"Felyx said in the video that he thinks Isaac Banewind is still alive," Katie says. "You think that's true, Jensen?"

"I don't know how that would be possible. But if it is, then that means the Banewind lineage would still exist. Which could potentially pose a huge threat to the Voidweavers."

"But why?" I say.

He shrugs. "They were a well-liked family. I'm sure they would have all the power, support, and aid of the people. They were the only known Formulists who could dual-wield fire and ice magic. So if they're still around, maybe the Voidweavers fear they could lose again."

"I feel like we just keep getting more questions, with no answers," I say. "What do we even do at this point?"

"Keep making sure you're safe," Jensen says. "Hopefully, Sadie can recruit more help from the Council with all the information we know now. We just have to avoid the Magician, Valkryn, and Scythe."

"I still don't know about Scythe." I sigh. "I'm not convinced he's bad."

"Well, either way, we have to keep our guard up." He looks at Katie. "And I know you told Katie about this, and I understand why you did. But I think the less people who know, the better."

"Oh, um, yeah." I bite my lip. "I kinda confronted my dad about it this morning."

"Genevieve!" Katie and Jensen say, in unison.

"He's not going to tell anyone. He doesn't know any more than what Sadie had already told us. My mother kept him in the dark, too."

Jensen nods. "Okay. Well, at least you ripped that bandage off. How did he handle it?"

"I probably shouldn't have told him before heading off to school. But now he knows and can let it sink in before we discuss it again."

The warning bell rings for the next period.

"Shoot, we're going to be late for class." Katie looks up at the clock. "Okay, guys, I'm glad we got to chat. I feel much better. Thank you."

"Yeah, same," I say. "Maybe this is all going to work out okay."

Not sure I believe that.

16

MISSING

THE NEXT MORNING, I WAKE UP EARLIER THAN USUAL, finding it difficult to sleep after the events of the last several days.

"Where's Dad?" Danny grabs the milk from the refrigerator.

Unlike my father, I refuse to cater to my little brother when it comes to meals. The farthest I'll go is setting out cereal boxes for him to choose.

"He had to go in early for conferences, remember? I'm driving you to school today when I leave."

I'm grateful that my father's been so busy with work, because I have not had to further discuss with him my current situation.

"Ugh. But I'll be there too early." He groans, dropping his forehead against the refrigerator door. "Why can't I just take the bus?"

"Because Dad doesn't trust you to get off to school by yourself." I wink at him. "And neither do I."

"Eh, yeah, I guess I don't, either."

I smile at him as I finish my glass of orange juice.

It isn't long before we are outside his school.

"Okay, I'll pick you up. Just hangout and chill until

I'm here." I roll down the passenger window as he steps out.

He frowns. "Why can't I walk home with Nick?"

"What?"

"It's Wednesday, remember? Nick usually walks home because the babysitter doesn't get there till later to let him in."

"Oh. Uh, sure. Just come right home, okay?"

"Yep. See ya." He turns and walks away, but within seconds halts and does a one-eighty back to the car. "And Genevieve?" An impish grin spreads across his face. "Would you mind taking care of Grendel again today? Pleeeeeeease?"

"Yeah, fine. Whatever." I'm secretly happy that I can take some time to play with the pupperino. "But you're washing my car twice!"

I hear him snickering as he runs off towards his group of friends.

"What an ass," I whisper, and catch myself smiling in the rearview mirror.

"Good morning, girls," the substitute teacher says, as Katie and I take our seats. "How are you this morning?"

"Great." Katie turns to me. "Wait. Where's Jensen and Sadie?"

As if on cue, Katie's phone vibrates.

"Oh! He just texted me."

"What's it say?"

She frowns as she turns the phone for me to see.

The Council wouldn't listen to Sadie yesterday. They've asked to meet with her again this morning, and want me to come along. I'll be back before the end of the day.

"That's disappointing." I sigh. "I don't understand why they're giving them such a hard time."

"Well, maybe Jensen's dad will be able to help convince them. I'm hopeful it'll work. Also, you need to get a new phone soon."

"Yeah, I know, I know. I can't wait for this week to be over."

I head home when school is finished, and grab the neighbor's keys from the bowl in the foyer. I see Danny's backpack resting on the kitchen chair, but there's no sign of him. I'm sure he's over playing with Nick, so I'll just get him at dinner time. Hey, it's easier on me not having to deal with him for the afternoon.

"Hi, you big lug," I coo at Grendel, as I enter the house.

He rolls onto his back and exposes his stomach.

"Oh, okay. I know what you want." I scratch his belly.

His leg kicks wild with excitement.

"How about I just let you out in the backyard this time, huh?"

I think back to last week when I went on a walk with him. The event that started all of this...

Grendel is jumping at the patio door before I can even get there to open it.

"Whoa there, boy. Calm down."

He whimpers as I unlock the kick plate.

I giggle. "For such a giant dog, you really are a big baby."

He lunges outside, barking as he rushes the squirrel sitting on the wooden fence. I follow him out and sit on the patio chair. The sun's rays feel good against my face. I close my eyes and listen to the breeze, the sound of Grendel walking through the grass, the birds chirping as they fly about the neighborhood. I take a deep breath, trying to clear my mind...to not have it racing for just a few moments.

"You certainly look peaceful for a girl who's being hunted down." Scythe's voice breaks through my serenity.

I snap my eyes snap open. He's standing over me, still wearing the blue track suit I've come to associate with him.

My heart sinks as I look at his face.

"Oh, Scythe," I whisper, and stand up from the chair as I remember the fight he and Jensen had.

His split lip is red and inflamed against his ashen skin, and numerous scrapes and bruises litter his cheeks and forehead. His swollen left eye is dark purple, obscuring the deep blue color that can usually be seen.

I reach my hand out and brush his cheek. He winces and pulls away.

"I'm fine." He looks at the ground and smiles. "I've had worse."

I stand there, not sure what to say.

"So..." He claps to get Grendel's attention.

The dog makes a run for him and jumps into his arms. Scythe scratches the beast's gigantic head.

"Jensen has left you alone again?" He laughs as Grendel's tongue splatters across his face.

He has a nice laugh, warm and inviting.

"He and Sadie are meeting with the Council."

Not sure if I should be telling him that.

"Oh?" He moves away from Grendel, crosses his arms, and shakes his black bangs out of his eyes. "Anything particular going on?"

I sigh. "I don't really know."

"Gotcha." He shifts his weight.

"They think you had something to do with the Magician finding me at the cemetery. But I'm not so sure."

He frowns. "I told you I didn't. Why else would I have gone over to Sadie's? I wanted you to know that it wasn't me. I was set up."

"But then, how did you know?"

He shakes his head and sighs. "There's a Formulist being kept as a prisoner in the Void Keep. He's part of the Council. His name is Mengurion Maldridge."

I jump. "Wait. I know who that is. He's the one who told Jensen and Sadie about me, warning them that the Voidweavers were trying to capture me."

"Yeah, that's him. He told me about you and your mother, about the Voidweavers and what they had done." Scythe drops down on the nearby patio chair. "I didn't want to be a part of it anymore."

"I don't understand." I sit next to him. "If you don't want to be a Voidweaver, then why are you working with them?"

"I didn't have a choice." His voice cracks. "My family died when I was ten years old. I was placed in the orphanage because no one else would take me in. I can't even remember my parents. I remember nothing about my old life. The Voidweavers adopted me. They do that— recruit orphans to train in their army. I was young, and I didn't have a choice. Plus, it was better than being alone in the Orphanotrophium. That place...it's enough to make anyone want to die."

"So you've been with the Voidweavers this whole time?" I feel myself sympathizing with him. "Have you ever learned more about your real family?"

He casts his gaze to the ground. "I don't even know my real name."

"What?"

He pulls off his blue jacket and turns around, lifting his black T-shirt to reveal his porcelain-white skin. His spine is prominent, and spanning the entirety of his back is a crescent-shaped scar.

"They called me Scythe because they said that's what my scar resembled. I don't know how I got it." He pulls his shirt back down and puts on his jacket. "Mengurion Maldridge told me that if I helped him, I could learn about my real family. I could escape the life I've come to know." He sniffles, wiping his eyes with the back of his hand. "So I said yes." He shakes his head. "The Magician must have known I was distancing myself from him. I thought I was being careful when I went to meet you at the cemetery... but he still managed to follow me. I'm sorry."

I sit there listening to his story, unsure what comforting words I can offer. He has known nothing but pain and suffering his entire life, and here he we were assuming everything that was incorrect about him.

I reach out and pat his knee. "Scythe, it's okay. You don't need to apologize. You didn't do anything wrong. But why didn't you tell us this when I first met you?"

"Maldridge asked me not to. He said it could risk everything if anyone who wasn't supposed to know found out. But I'm telling you now because I need you to trust me. I need to find out about my family, and I want to help save you, too."

I sit in silence.

"Why don't we put the dog back inside and head over to my place?" I finally say. "I'm starving and could definitely eat something. We can talk more there."

He smiles weakly. "Sounds good to me."

After giving Grendel a treat and refilling his water bowl, we leave through the garage. I punch in the number on the keypad to put down the door, and tap my foot against the driveway as I wait for it to shut.

"So where have you been staying while you're in town?" I cross my arms as we walk back towards my house, and wonder if he realizes how awkward I feel talking to him.

"Just here and there."

I wait for him to continue, but he doesn't say anything.

As we enter my yard, I see Nick playing basketball by himself next door.

"That's odd."

Nick's shot bounces off the backboard.

"Wonder why isn't he playing with my brother."

I continue past our house, towards Nick. When he sees us approaching, he picks up the ball and smiles at us.

"Hi, Genevieve!" His blond hair sits disheveled on top of his head. "What's up?"

"Hi, Nick. I was just coming to check on Danny. Is he inside?"

"I dunno." Nick shrugs. "He was supposed to go drop off his stuff and come back over to play, but he hasn't yet. I thought the babysitter went with him."

"When was this?" My heart beats faster. "Nick, when?"

"Right when we got home from school. Like an hour ago, maybe? Why? What's wrong?"

"He wasn't in the house." I turn to Scythe, my stomach tying into knots. "His backpack was in the kitchen, but he wasn't there."

"Genevieve? Is he okay?" Nick says.

Fear creeps over his young face.

"I'm sure he's fine, Nick." I reach out to touch his shoulder. "Why don't you go back inside your house and play some video games, all right? I'll tell Danny to come back over later tonight." I turn back towards my house.

"What are you thinking?" Scythe follows next to me.

My heart is beating behind my ears.

"I don't know, but something's not right."

Danny does a lot of stupid things, but leaving the house on his own isn't one of them.

"Danny!" I rush through the front door, run upstairs and into his bedroom.

Empty.

"Is he there?" I barrel down the stairs.

"No," Scythe says, from the family room.

I open the basement door, to darkness.

"Danny!" I'm almost crying.

Scythe comes up behind me and grabs my shoulders.

"Genevieve, calm down. Take a deep breath."

"I-I...where is he?" My vision is blurred with tears. "He should be here. He wouldn't just leave. Something's wrong, Scythe. Something is very wrong."

I jump as a cell phone's chime rips through the air.

Scythe grabs the phone from his pocket. "Hello?"

His face hardens, and his lips carve into a frown. He lowers the phone from his ear and presses the speakerphone button.

"Am I on? Can you hear me?"

A chill runs down my spine as I recognize the voice.

"We're here," Scythe says.

"Ah, excellent," the Magician says. "I was worried I wouldn't catch you."

"Where's my brother?" I hiss, trying to choke back my tears. "What have you done with him?"

"Okay, Genevieve," the Magician growls. "You want to play now? Let's play. Your brother is with me. At the old church. Scythe knows the one. And if you aren't here in the next ten minutes, I will kill him. Do you understand?"

I crash into the foyer table, scrambling to grab my car keys from the bowl. I knock it to the floor, but barely register the sound as it shatters to pieces. I throw open the door and race toward the car. My vision tunnels. Chest pounds. Breath shallow and spastic.

Seconds later, I'm fumbling with the car handle, trying to pull open the driver's door.

"Genevieve. Stop!" Scythe shouts.

"Get in."

He groans, but opens the passenger door and slides in.

"Drive that way." He points.

We're blasting down the road. I see the speedometer climb. 40. 50. 60. The neighborhood houses zoom by, their normally vibrant hues blurred together into an ugly dark pallet.

"Genevieve!" A car horn blares as we speed through a stop sign.

"He's going to kill my brother! He's going to kill Danny!"

"This is a trap, Genevieve. He knows he can use your brother against you. He—"

"I don't care, Scythe. He *can* use my brother against me. Screw the trap. He. Has. My. Brother."

Scythe's phone rings. I answer.

"How are you feeling, Miss DeWinter?" The Magician's words fill the car. "It's kind of riveting, isn't it?

The adrenaline rush you're experiencing."

"Please, don't hurt Danny. Please. I'll talk to you or whoever else you need me to talk to. Just don't hurt my brother."

"That's completely in your hands, my dear. Are you getting close? Because according to my watch, you only have about thirty seconds left."

"Scythe!"

"We're almost there," he says, through gritted teeth. "Turn here!"

"Poor boy." The Magician sighs. "He doesn't even know how he ended up in this whole mess. What fortuitous circumstances. Oh, fifteen seconds now."

The car decelerates at an alarming rate as I slam on the brakes and veer and skid into the church's expansive driveway. The smell of burning rubber stings my nostrils as the vehicle rumbles across the gravel, jarring us to a stop.

"Ten seconds."

I fling open the car door.

"Genevieve. No!" Scythe's words echo past my ears.

The abandoned church towers over me.

"Five seconds, Miss DeWinter."

I'm still holding the phone. Focused on nothing but my brother.

"Four."

I leap up the cement stairs, two at a time.

"Three."

I reach out and grab the ornamental door handles.

"Two."

The door creaks open.

"One."

I sprint inside.

"See you soon, Miss DeWinter."

I'm not even halfway down the main aisle when a blinding light engulfs me, crushing me like a giant vice. I feel the familiar pull as my body is tugged into another dimension, tearing me from this earth.

And then all goes black.

17

SMASH!

MY HEAD...

The pain is excruciating, gripping my skull like a steel vice.

"Ah, Miss DeWinter. We were hoping you'd be joining us soon."

I slowly open my eyes, waiting for the black spots to clear from my vision. An orange blob appears in front of me, coming into focus as I regain clarity.

The Magician stares at me with a sadistic grin.

"Welcome to my lab."

The room is dimly lit by purple lighting, radiating down from the dome-shaped ceiling. My hands are chained above my head, and my feet just barely touch the concrete floor. I turn my neck and see Scythe next to me, in the same position. He's staring blankly ahead, his eyes empty hollows.

The Magician walks over to a table and picks up an odd-looking object that resembles a lantern. On the wall is mounted a large tool board with instruments of various shapes and sizes. He scans over each item before grabbing a crescent-shaped knife.

I want to say something to Scythe, but can't find my voice.

The Magician moves back towards us.

"I'm going to tell you a little story." He takes off his orange, pointed hat and places in on a stool next to him. "Because when you get right down to it, we really don't know each other that well, do we?"

"Where's my brother?" I manage to whisper.

My throat feels like sandpaper.

"He's preoccupied at the moment." The Magician rolls his eyes. "And before you ask...no. I didn't kill him... yet."

"Where are we?" Scythe says.

"We're in the Void Keep. Now ask another question, and I'll cut your tongue out." The Magician flashes the knife at us. "You see, after the fall of Ganstin Remores, our Void King, most of our followers were scattered to the winds—scared into hiding, arrested and imprisoned, murdered. They were broken and downtrodden. Without the Void King, there was very little hope of us being restored to the power we once were. But with the leadership and guidance of the Dark Lady, we glued back the pieces, one splinter at a time. And then it all changed. The Dark Lady found out that our Void King might not truly be dead. It was surmised that he was alive, sealed away in an eternal abyss. Of course, it was your mother's power that forever cursed him, locking him away, enslaved to her will. So it made sense that the only way to undo the spell would be to use an entity similar to the one that had initially imprisoned him. And then the Dark Lady learned that Addisyn DeWinter had a daughter." He sneers at me, his stained teeth gleaming in the purple light. "Well, you know how the story goes from there. And here we are." He frowns at Scythe. "And this one. Well, we were foolish to recruit his help. He came to the Voidweavers years ago, joining the other youths in the Orphanotrophium. The goal was always to rehabilitate the adolescents into soldiers for the Dark Lady's army. But Scythe never had...potential." The Magician scoffs. "At best, we thought he could help us find you. And if he got killed along the way, no one would care. But he did find you. Took him a couple months, but he did. Isn't that right, Scythe?"

Scythe sways from the metal chains, his gaze fixed on the floor below him.

"The problem is that he fell in love with you." The Magician guffaws. "As if the boy even knows what that word means. He hasn't experienced love his entire life. Ah, but I guess following someone around for several months will do that to you."

"If my mother is still alive, why haven't you gone after her?" I glare at the Magician.

"A damn fine question, Genevieve. Good for you." He stalks forward, extending the knife toward my chest. "Unfortunately, we don't have time to discuss that issue right now."

"Don't you dare hurt her!" Scythe writhes next to me. "Don't you touch her!"

My heart beats faster as the Magician curls the metal blade under my shirt's neck collar, pushing my mother's necklace out of the way and slicing through the cotton like butter. The material falls forward, exposing my upper chest. I squeeze my eyes shut, my breaths shallow and rapid.

"Shh. Calm down, Genevieve, it's okay," the Magician whispers into my ear.

I feel his hot breath creep across my skin.

"I just need a little bit of your blood, that's all."

"Stop. No!" Scythe snarls, thrashing his chains.

The Magician places the knife's edge against my skin, carving into me with a slow, steady motion. I cringe as the metal cuts deep into my flesh, sending a jolt of pain through my body. My eyes are shut tight, the tears burning my cheeks as they force through. A warm liquid drips down my chest.

"This device I've created," the Magician places the lantern underneath the flowing blood, "can distinguish what type of Formulist a person is." He presses hard on my collarbone to milk even more blood. "Ergo, if our dear Genevieve truly is a paladin, this will let us know. There. All done."

He tightens the top of the device and places it on his lab bench. The glass windows are splattered with blood, and the red liquid is sloshing around at the container's bottom. He presses a button at its base and the machine whirs to life, working itself up until it's spinning so fast that the blood is nothing but a red blur.

"Just have to wait a few minutes now." The Magician sneers. "I'm sure the anticipation is killing us all."

Clang, clang, clang! The sharp metal knocks reverberate around the room.

"Yes?" The Magician turns toward the steel door.

It slowly swings open, revealing the young man who'd helped me escape from Banewind just days before.

"Ah, Kingston," the Magician mumbles. "I was hoping the Dark Lady would be down to check on us."

"Sorry to disappoint." Kingston's black armor sparkles in the room's light. "How's it going in here?"

I shudder as his haunting gaze makes contact with mine, the white glow of his eyes reflecting their mysterious aura in the dim room. His white hair is styled neatly to the side, with a few escaped strands dangling over his forehead. He pays no attention to Scythe, nor me.

"I'm testing her blood now." The Magician motions to the device. "We'll soon know whether this entire goose chase was worth it or not."

"I see." Kingston walks over to a stack of steel rods leaning against the wall. "Have you spoken to Valkryn yet?"

"She was taking the girl's brother down to the Prison Ward." The Magician strokes his black goatee. "But that's as much as I know."

"Gotcha." Kingston places his black gauntlet on one of the rods and spins it against the floor. "And what about Scythe?"

"Eh, I don't know." The Magician frowns and turns back around to face us, moving closer to Scythe. "I'm hoping they have no need for him now. I could always use another subject for Project Corlynnia."

Click! The machine slows down.

"Well?" Kingston moves towards the lab bench. "What happened?"

"It...no..." The Magician places his hand against the lantern. "Nothing happened. There was no reaction." He turns around and glares at me. "She isn't a paladin! She has no Formulist's blood in her at all." His nostrils flare. "She's nothing but a stupid gir—"

Kingston plunges the rod into the Magician's back until it explodes out through his chest. I scream as blood projects across the room, speckling my face and body. The Magician lurches forward, blood seeping from his mouth as he sputters for breath. Kingston retracts the rod, and the Magician crumples to his knees.

"You may want to look away." Kingston keeps

his gaze on the Magician and reels the rod around like a baseball bat to slam it into the side of the Magician's face.

The sound of bones splintering resonates through my ears as his body crumples to the floor.

The bloodied rod drops from Kingston's grip and clangs on the ground next to the mangled corpse.

He looks at me and grins. "You have no idea how long I've been wanting to do that. Now let's get you two out of here."

18

THE PRISON WARD

PARALYZED. MY BODY, MY VOICE, MY MIND.

I'm staring at Kingston in front of me and see the Magician's corpse strewn across the floor, but I don't register it. Every inch of me is paralyzed. Numb. Broken.

"Go grab that towel." Kingston breaks Scythe from the chains.

His voice sounds distant, muffled, as if I'm hearing it from underwater.

My body lifts into the air as Kingston tugs on my chains. They tighten, snap, and then my arms fall forward meeting no resistance. My legs are limp, and I feel like I'm watching myself from outside my body as Kingston helps lower me onto the ground.

Scythe takes the towel and wipes away the warm blood speckled across my face. I see the red pool expanding across the floor.

"Is she okay?" he says.

"Yeah, she's fine. She's just in shock." Kingston continues to hold me in his arms, rubbing my back. "Genevieve, try and take a couple deep breaths. Genevieve." He turns my face towards his.

Again I notice how beautiful he is, with his glowing white eyes and high-set cheekbones.

"Genevieve, just look at me." He smiles.

All at once, my senses return and I can't help but scream. Kingston clamps his hand over my mouth.

"You're going to have to not do that." He traps my voice until I fall silent. "You okay now?"

Scythe is standing over me, too, his face painted with concern.

I nod. Kingston releases his hand.

"Here, let's get you to your feet." He looks at one of the workbenches. "Go grab that blanket, Scythe. Throw it over his body."

He does so.

"There. All better." Kingston moves away from me, but still remains guarded, his hands nearby in case I falter in my steps.

"I'm okay now," I whisper, my voice shaking. "I just...I wasn't expecting that to happen."

"Neither was I." Scythe glares at Kingston. "I'm not sure I understand what's going on."

"Yes, I would imagine you wouldn't. But you guys are okay. The Magician is dead, and we can get you out of here. I just need to find where he put the portal key."

"What are you talking about? I have to go get my brother!" A wave of fear crashes into me with the remembrance of Danny. "We're wasting time standing around here."

"Are you stupid?" Kingston gawks at me, his eyes bulging. "Really, Genevieve. Are you *that* dumb?"

"What the hell is wrong with you?" I hiss. "My brother is about to be killed, and you just want me to leave? Are *you* stupid, Kingston?"

"Genevieve, you're testing my patience." He scoffs, reaching under the blood-soaked sheet to check the Magician's pockets.

"Scythe?"

"If we go search for your brother, there is a very good chance that we may end up dead ourselves." He glances at Kingston and looks back at me. "We're not going to be saved every time."

"I know that." I bite my lip, trying to hold back my tears as I gaze at Scythe. "But I'm not losing any more family members. Not like this."

Scythe sighs.

"Got it." Kingston stands back up. "Go get over on the platform."

"The Prison Ward isn't far from here," Scythe says. "We can go together. If that's really what you want to do." He frowns at Kingston. "She will never forgive any of us if we don't try."

Kingston slams the portal key onto the table.

"You both disgust me," he growls. "Why can neither of you make things easy?" He stalks toward the door. "What are you going to do about the security system, Scythe? There are cameras everywhere."

"Uhh..."

"Yeah, didn't think about that one, did you?"

I look from Scythe to Kingston, waiting for one of them to say something.

Kingston sighs. "Luckily for you two, I disabled the cameras before coming here." He heads toward the door, but pauses. "And for the record, Scythe killed the Magician after he escaped from his chains." He squints at us. "Isn't that right?"

"Absolutely." Scythe looks at me.

"I don't know how else it could have happened."

"Good," Kingston says. "Then grab the portal key, and let's go."

We disappear into the black corridor.

"I would have expected more guards in a place like this," I whisper, as we continue to wind through the maze of halls.

The dim lighting casts my shadow against the wall's black stones, and it flickers with the motion of my movements.

"That's because they're all at an assembly." Kingston eyes me with disapproval. "So I would suggest we get this done quickly, before it concludes."

"It's gonna be okay," Scythe says, next to my ear, and wraps his cold fingers around my hand to give me a gentle squeeze. "This will be over soon."

I tighten my grip around his hand, then quickly let go.

We round the corner, and two guards are standing before us, positioned in front of a purple steel door.

Kingston jars to a halt. "Good afternoon, gentlemen."

I stand there next to Scythe, frozen. We both glance at each other before focusing our attention back on the two men dressed in black armor.

"Not at the assembly, I see?" Kingston says.

"Commander Starmantle!" One of the guards bows toward Kingston. "Good to see you, sir. We were told to remain stationed here. Were we given the wrong orders?"

"No, no. You're fine." Kingston looks back at us. "I'm just here to lock up these two."

"Oh?" The guard peers at me from under his helmet.

I try to avoid his gaze.

"Yes, there's been... an incident." Kingston grabs Scythe by his jacket collar and tugs him out in front. "This one has killed Blaine Fortrunner."

The other guard gasps. "The Magician?"

Kingston nods. "Yeah, I know." He gestures to the door. "Do you know if my mother's still in there?"

I do a double-take. *Mother? Wait, what?*

The guard shakes his head. "Lady Salharia left not too long ago. I believe she was on her way to the assembly to join the Dark Lady."

"Perfect. She doesn't need to concern herself with this right now. I'll talk to her later."

"Absolutely, Commander. Anything else?"

"Just open the Prison Ward for us."

The purple door churns as it rises into the air.

"Thank you, gentlemen." Kingston motions for us to follow him inside. "Do you know where she locked up the young boy?"

"Block five, row D, cell thirty-one."

As we enter, the door lowers behind us.

Kingston turns around and nods at the guards. "See you later."

Boom! The sound reverberates around the Prison Ward as the door settles, locking us inside.

"Whoa," I take in my surroundings.

The Prison Ward is expansive, with vaulted ceilings illuminated by bright fluorescent lighting. The room seems to stretch on into the distance forever, with countless rows running out into an endless horizon, all lined by cells on each side.

We enter one of the rows, and I can see several prisoners locked behind their cells. There are no metal bars or doors containing them, but only a translucent pink veil separating the prisoners from us. A soft static hums as we pass each cell, and flickers of electricity spark across the pink reflective screens. I feel like I've walked right into some sort of futuristic space film.

"For a brief moment, I thought about killing those guards." Kingston's white teeth dazzle as his smirk widens. "But then I realized that couldn't fit into a story anyway I tried spinning it."

"Um, yeah. About that." I stop and wait until he turns around and looks at me. "Your *mother*, Kingston? Who is your mother?"

He scoffs and continues walking. "Not the time nor the place, Genevieve."

I turn toward Scythe. "Well?"

He shakes his head and sighs. "Kingston's mother is Valkryn."

He tries to pass me, but I shoot my hand out and clutch his arm.

"Excuse me?" I stare at Scythe. "She's what?"

Kingston is several feet ahead of us, but has again stopped.

"Is that true, Kingston?" I hiss, through grinded teeth. "Your mother is one of the women who has been trying to kill me?"

"The two of us hold very different viewpoints on a lot of things, Genevieve. It's a complicated issue."

"No. No, it's really not." My heartbeat quickens, and my palms start to sweat. "Telling me a whole other world exists beside my own...that's complicated. Explaining to me that my mother may still be alive...also a tricky situation. But knowing that *your* mother, your own living, breathing relative, is trying to kill me...well, that seems pretty straightforward. You either want someone dead or you don't," I growl at Kingston, my nostrils flaring. "So tell me how that is a *complicated* issue."

"Genevieve," Kingston snarls, his jaw clenched. "Shut the hell up and follow me to rescue your damn brother. Understand?"

"Oh, my, my, my, my." A voice echoes around us, the words lingering on my ears like mist. "Why such hostility, friends?"

The air stirs next to me, swirling into purple fog as it forms into a humanoid figure.

Naxxorius comes into view, his silver robes tumbling to the ground like moonlit waves. He hovers in place, floating next to Kingston.

"Quarreling will do nothing but impede your quest, ah?" Naxxorius turns his head toward me, and his purple essence dances inside his vessel as he bows. "Greetings, Lady Genevieve. How lovely it is to see you again. I did not believe it would be such a short time frame until our next encounter."

"Did Valkryn see you in here?" Kingston says.

"Of course not. I would never allow myself to get into such a situation. That's preposterous of you to even conceive."

Naxxorius glides down the row, and we follow him.

"So no one saw you come into the Keep?" Kingston says. "And you didn't try anything foolish?"

"Define foolish." Naxxorius chuckles. "Oh, lighten up, Kingston. Of course not. I'm simply doing an errand, for which you're paying me. No need to worry yourself."

"Kingston told you to come here?" I look over at him. "But that would mean you were already planning to help us."

Kingston remains silent.

"I don't get it. If you're a Voidweaver, why are you doing so much for me?"

"Perhaps you should not question Kingston's actions," Naxxorius says, "but merely appreciate that he is doing them, ah? Sometimes it is better to take the plain dish from the top than risk pulling out the ornate china from the bottom."

Before I can reply, we stop in front of a cell and I see Danny inside, lying on a stone slab.

"Danny!" I gasp, running towards the cell.

Kingston reaches his arm out in front of me and pulls me to a stop.

"You'll electrocute yourself if you touch the barrier." He holds me back.

After a moment, he lowers his arm, and I walk as close to the pink screen as I can. My brother's chest slowly rises up and down, and a peaceful look is spread across his face, as if he were merely at home taking a nap. He appears uninjured, with the only thing out of place being his messy brown hair spiked atop his head.

I pull my lips into a disheartened smile as a tight lump settles into my throat.

"Do you think he's all right?" I take one more glance at him before turning to Kingston. "You don't think they hurt him?"

He shakes his head. "No, he's fine. As a general rule, my mother doesn't hurt children."

"Oh, isn't that good of her."

Kingston sighs. "I'm not sure how to pull off this next part."

"What do you mean?" Scythe says.

"How to fake this." Kingston runs his hand through

his hair. "We obviously can't just let him out, or everyone is going to know you had some sort of help."

"Okay," I reply. "Sooooo..."

"I don't know. I was thinking we could blame Naxx?" He looks over at the elemental. "I don't suppose I could bribe you into that?"

"I offer my services when I can. But as you know, I will not break neutrality. That would damage my relationship with the Voidweavers, considerably. You understand, ah?"

"Yeah, whatever. Okay, well, then Scythe is going to have to attack me." Kingston pulls out his sword from its sheath, and the prison barrier's pink light reflects off the steel. "And we'll stage it that way."

"What? No. No way." Scythe backs away from the sword. "I'm not going to hurt you."

"Well what else do you want to do?" Kingston growls. "Come on. We don't have a lot of time here, people."

"Forgive me for intruding, but might I offer a suggestion?"

Scythe jumps, startled by the voice coming from the cell behind him.

A tall, elderly man approaches the pink barrier. His long white beard flows halfway down his chest, a stark contrast to the tattered beige robe draped over his gaunt figure. As he smiles at us, the creases around his soft gray eyes become more prominent, radiating a warm glow, even within the Prison Ward.

Kingston gasps. "Magister Maldridge. I apologize. I did not realize your cell was near here." He bows toward the old man.

The magister holds up his hand in protest. "Formalities are neither expected nor warranted, my dear boy." His gaze moves from Kingston to Naxxorius, and finally to Scythe. "I am glad to see you're all alive and well." As he looks at me, his smile widens even more. "Genevieve DeWinter." His voice is soft and light. "My, do you have your mother's beauty. My name is Mengurion Maldridge, and it is lovely to meet you." The smile fades, and his face hardens. "But there are more pressing matters at hand." He motions to my brother's cell. "Have Naxxorius disable the barrier and knock Kingston unconscious." He nods to Kingston. "You can tell your mother that you were going to put them in the same cell as her brother, when they caught you off-guard. There is no doubt she will be upset, but you are her son and she will forgive you." He looks back to Naxxorius. "You can help the three of them escape. Does someone have the portal key to return?"

"Yeah, I have it." Scythe pulls it out of his pocket.

"Excellent."

"What about you?" Kingston says. "You can get out, too."

"That will be an additional charge," Naxxorius says.

"Shut up, Naxx," Kingston snarls.

"No, I cannot go with you," the magister says. "There is no rationale for why I would have been let out, too. It will give you away."

"But—"

"No, Kingston. Think logically, remember?"

Kingston hesitates before straightening up. "I understand." He motions to Danny's cell. "All right, Naxx. Go ahead and—"

"What's going on here?" Valkryn's voice shatters the air, her words piercing like glass shards.

"Ah." Naxxorius fades away before Valkryn can see him.

Kingston steps out in front of Scythe and me, his

body rigid as he approaches his mother.

"Damnit!" he says. "I told the guards not to bother you. Everything's fine. I've got it under control."

"Do you?" Valkryn raises her silver eyebrows. "Because I was told that Blaine Fortrunner is dead."

"Yeah, well, there was an incident." Kingston motions to us. "But I was able to intervene."

Valkryn moves closer. Her green high-heeled boots echo rhythmically throughout the Prison Ward. For the first time, I can clearly make out the woman who has been trying to kill me. Her latex suit consists of two colors, black and amethyst, patterned so that one half of her upper body is the same color as the opposite leg. Her silver hair falls to her back in curls, causing her pale face to appear even whiter, and her toxic green lipstick stands out against her violet eyes.

As cold as she appears, I can't help but be mesmerized by her beauty. Her neck is supple, her cheekbones high set, and her face perfectly symmetrical.

She stops just inches from me.

"You have become quite the nuisance to me, Genevieve DeWinter."

Hearing my name spoken by her sounds odd, like foreign words I don't recognize.

"I certainly hope you're worth the trouble that the Dark Lady thinks you are."

"Well, I'm not." I stare back into her eyes.

I imagine she's about the same age my mother would be right now.

"Genevieve—"

"It's fine, Scythe." I keep eye contact with Valkryn. "Yeah, your magician friend did the test on me, and it turns out I'm not a paladin." I scoff. "In fact, I'm not even a Formulist at all."

She turns to Kingston. "Is this true?"

Kingston glares at me. "According to Fortrunner's machine, yes, that's right. She isn't a paladin. But the machine could be wrong. You know his projects aren't always perfect."

"Perhaps." Valkryn rubs the side of her face, and I see her nails are the same color as her lips. "And what about him?"

She's still focused on me, but her words make me look over to Scythe.

"What about him?" Kingston says.

"He's served his purpose, hasn't he? He got the girl to come here, despite that he has been utterly useless to us this entire time." She crosses her arms as she examines Scythe. "I'm assuming he's the one who killed the Magician?"

"Yes, but—"

"Then at this point, he's done more harm than good." She glares at Scythe. "We don't need him anymore."

"I know. That's why I brought them here. I was going to lock the two of them up with her broth—"

"She can stay. The Dark Lady is still going to want to question her, regardless of her utility as a Formulist. But him? You can just kill him."

"No!" I shout.

Valkryn points her hand at me, and a dark shadow wraps around my body. An excruciating spasm washes over me as my muscles tighten, contorting me into a rigid position. I can't move or speak.

"You already have your sword out, Kingston. I am telling you to dispose of him now."

He looks down at his sword, still unsheathed from when he was offering it to Scythe to attack him just minutes ago.

"Kingston, please. I'm exhausted." Valkryn rubs her forehead. "Don't make me do this. Don't put me into a worse mood."

He looks from the weapon to Scythe, who's just standing there.

I want to scream. Yell. Punch and claw and cry.

Run away! Please just run away. Run!

Scythe looks over his shoulder at Mengurion Maldridge, who is still observing all this from his cell. He has a stoic look on his face, his lips pressed together as he stares back at Scythe.

I don't know whether or not he's surprised by what's happening, but Scythe turns to me. And even amongst the bruises and cuts scattered across his face, the swollen cheek, the blackened eye, and that he's trapped here in the Prison Ward because of my brother, he smiles.

And at that moment, I realize this boy, who I've hardly known, is willing to die for me.

Swoooooooosh!

The sword's steel pierces the air before penetrating Scythe's abdomen. I watch in horror as Kingston steps closer, twisting the weapon deeper into his body.

Scythe gasps, his eyes wide as blood erupts from his mouth. He falls forward into Kingston, who lowers him to the ground as he retracts his sword. The pool of blood shimmers across the floor, reflecting the barrier's pink light as it pours from Scythe's body.

My heart is racing. Head pounding. Breath feels like fire burning through my lungs.

But I'm still frozen in place.

Blood gurgles from Scythe's mouth as his gasps become shallower. Kingston stands and wipes his sword across Scythe's clothes before placing it back in its sheath.

"Go get the Dark Lady," Valkryn tells Kingston, paying no attention to Scythe's bloodied body. "I'll handle the girl."

Kingston glances at me before heading back down the hallway. Scythe's body is now lying motionless on the ground.

Valkryn nudges him with her boot.

"Well, Genevieve," she flicks her hand at me, and my body melts from its pose as I crumble to the ground, "it looks like your friend is gone."

My face is pressed against the cold concrete, inches away from the blood that's still spreading. Its smell is strong in my nostrils, and I feel my tears well-up as I match my gaze with Scythe's lifeless eyes.

He's dead, Genevieve. He's dead, and soon you are going to be, too.

19

RIVALRY

KINGSTON MOVES THROUGH THE VOID KEEP'S CORRIDORS, and stops in front of a sewer grate secured into the stonewall. The ground is damp under his feet, and his heels dig into the loose cement as he tightens his grip around the steel bars, pulling the grate away. Water echoes through the darkness as a cold breeze dances through his white hair.

Jensen Saint Clair emerges from the drain, dressed in his red cloak.

"Thanks." He pulls down his hood.

"You sure no one saw you?"

Jensen answers with a glare.

"I just had to ask." Kingston closes the grate.

"How long have they been here for?" Jensen pulls his phone from his pocket to check the time.

"I don't know. Since a little bit after I called you. I tried to get ahold of you the minute I knew what was going on."

"Yeah, that's so sweet of you. Where are they now?"

"In the Prison Ward." Kingston shuffles his feet. "Jensen, things have happened..."

"What? Is Genevieve all right?" His voice rises.

Kingston nods. "Yes. Well, right now, anyway. She's with my mother."

"Are you serious? And you think *that's* all right? This is unbelievable. How could you even—"

"The Magician is dead. So is Scythe."

Jensen stares at Kingston, his brown eyes fogged with confusion.

"What?"

"Later, okay? You need to just get there and stop Valkryn from doing whatever she wants to do. Follow this hallway until you see the big purple door. I texted you the code. I'll stall on my way to the Dark Lady."

"Yeah, okay." Jensen starts to walk away.

"What? Not even a *thank you* for my help?"

"Really?" Jensen scoffs. "You really think I should thank you for all this?"

"I think without my help, Genevieve would have already been dead by this point." Kingston steps toward Jensen. "But you just don't want to admit that because it would make you seem weak."

"Wow, Starmantle. Sadie and I had this situation handled fine. It was *you* who decided to interfere."

"I only did what your brother asked me to do. And when you think about it, how many days was I the one keeping an eye on Genevieve? Huh? While you or Sadie were running around doing whatever it was you guys were doing. It really says a lot that Casius didn't trust you to handle this, doesn't it?"

"Shut up," Jensen growls. "You don't know what you're talking about."

"I don't understand why you dislike me so much. I

have done everything to show my loyalty to your family, and yet you treat me like I'm going to turn around and stab all of you in the back. Do you know how many times I've risked my life for you guys?"

"I don't care how much you do for us. And I don't care how much you claim to love my brother. The fact of the matter is you are Kingston Starmantle, son of Valkryn Salharia, Second Commander to the Dark Lady's Void Knights. And that is never going to change."

Kingston laughs. "Ah, see, so this is about Casius and me." He shakes his head. "You can't stand that your brother and I are still in a relationship."

"It has nothing to do with that. It's completely separate from the politics happening in Banewind. You are a Voidweaver, and when it comes down to it, I know you would kill my brother and family if you had to save your—"

Kingston lashes his hand out and wraps it around Jensen's neck. The metal gauntlet tightens as Kingston raises him into the air. Jensen gasps, sputtering for breath.

"You don't know the first thing about what I would or would not do for Casius," Kingston snarls. "I would never let harm come to him or the family."

"And yet...here I am...choking by your hand." Jensen wheezes, pulling at Kingston's gauntlet.

He falls to the floor once Kingston releases him.

Booooooooooooooooom!

The hallway rumbles as dust from the ceiling falls to the floor.

Kingston looks at Jensen. "You need to go. Now."

Jensen rubs his throat as he stands, and brushes off his cloak.

"I'll hold off the Dark Lady as long as I can," Kingston says. "But once you have Genevieve, get out."

"Yeah, I got it. Thanks." Jensen coughs out the words.

Kingston nods before the two of them run off in opposite directions.

20

NEW TRICKS

I STARE AT SCYTHE'S BODY.

Motionless. Breathless. Lifeless.

Dead.

The blood continues to spread across the floor, slowing now. My mind is numb, my legs paralyzed. I'm just sitting here, unaware of anything else around me.

There's a muffled voice. "S-------"

My pulse is bounding behind my ears, rushing past my eyes.

"St-----!"

I'm looking past Scythe. I can see Maldridge in his prison cell. And a shadow looming near me. I remember it belongs to—

"Stand up!" Valkryn kicks me in the side with her boot.

My body restarts, as though an electrical current has sparked through every inch of my being.

"You killed him!" I jump to my feet. "You killed him!" I glare at Valkryn, irate at the smug look spreading across her face.

"I like this side of you, Genevieve. It's nice to see a

girl with bite." She chomps her teeth, winking at me.

I approach Scythe's body and bend down to place my hand on his head. My vision blurs, the tears hot on my cheeks.

"Oh, please. Don't get all sentimental." Valkryn walks over to my brother's cell and punches in a number on the keypad.

The barrier disappears as I hear the electricity whirring down.

"He really wasn't worth getting all bent out of shape over."

"I'm so sorry, Scythe," I whisper, rubbing his black hair, grasping at the strands between my fingers. "I did this to you." I place my hand over his heart, his blood-soaked shirt cool beneath my touch.

"People die, Genevieve." She crosses her arms as she leans against the cell. "You get used to it. No matter who it is."

I close Scythe's eyelids.

"All right." Valkryn inhales deeply as she nods to the cell. "In you go."

I lock my gaze with hers.

"Let my brother go," I whisper, "and I'll get in."

"No, this isn't a negotiation." She turns toward Danny. "Although, I do feel bad we've pulled your brother into this for nothing now. My philosophy is never to harm children." She clicks her tongue. "But I can't say the Dark Lady feels the same." She pivots around to face me. "You're sure you aren't a Formulist?"

"What? Are you serious?"

Valkryn shrugs. "Blaine has been known to...miss the mark on a few things. You do know why they call him the Magician, don't you?"

I turn back to Scythe, still resting my hand on his chest.

"Blaine Fortrunner was actually an engineer by trade. His entire life, he was always tinkering with toys and building things. He came from a family that...wasn't the most supportive. His parents were never there for him. He had no siblings, no friends. And no one cared about his hobbies or interests. He just simply existed. But somehow he got through all that and was accepted into the Academy to pursue his passions and dreams. He believed he'd find himself surrounded by individuals of the same intellectual caliber, but he quickly learned the world was just as cruel wherever you went. For most of his schooling, he was ridiculed for the ideas and projects he tried to develop. Many of them never worked. And when they did, people would just snicker and say it was from sheer luck. Magic. The Magician had pulled off another trick. But what they didn't realize, Genevieve, was that his projects never worked because he was always striving for the unimaginable. He would tap into the mind's power, which the vast majority of the world was not yet ready for. And he didn't know it until he discovered the Voidweavers. Ganstin Remores, our Void King, he showed Fortrunner his true potential. And then you know what he did, Genevieve?" Her violet eyes are glowing, wide with excitement. "The Magician killed every last person who ever doubted him. Including his own parents. He didn't need them now. The Voidweavers were his new family. He had finally found what he'd always wanted."

"You're crazy," I whisper. "All of you."

"Perhaps." Valkryn laughs. "But at least we understand greatness requires sacrifice." She steps towards me. "Now get into the cell."

"Kill me. I don't care." I grimace, watching my hand tremble on Scythe's chest. "I'm done running from you."

"It's not my decision whether you live or die, Genevieve. That would be—"

"Yeah, I know," I snarl. "The Dark Lady. I get it." I climb to my feet. "It's amazing all the things I've heard about her, and yet she's never been brave enough to come get me herself."

"Don't—"

"What? Don't what? Talk about her? Speak her name? Mock her?" I laugh. "You seriously think I care about offending *you*? Yeah, okay."

"Genevieve. Get in the cell." Valkryn's pale face flushes as her nostrils flare.

"Why don't you use one of your little spells to paralyze me again?" I move closer to her. "Isn't that what you do, Valkryn? Control through fear?"

"Come here!" Valkryn reaches out to grab my shoulder.

I raise my hand to knock her out of the way.

But that isn't what happens.

Crack! A flash of light.

I close my eyes, caught off-guard by the dazzling glow. When I reopen them, I see Valkryn lying on the floor, several feet from me.

"You...you..." Her eyes are wide with astonishment. "You *are* a paladin."

I look down at my hand. A golden light engulfs my fist, moving like the oscillating waves of an ocean.

What the hell? I stand frozen.

My gaze shifts from my hand to Valkryn. She's now crouched on her feet, ready to pounce like a rabid dog. My heart's pounding against my chest. Body shaking.

I look at Maldridge. The only sound is the soft humming of the prison's many cells.

I head for my brother's cell.

"No!" Valkryn's shouts.

A shadow erupts beneath my feet.

Whack!

"Ugh!" I groan, as the air is knocked from my lungs, throwing me from his cell.

The shadow thrusts into my stomach, flinging me backward and slamming me down onto the concrete floor. I stare at the ceiling. Dazed. Gasping for air. Wheezing.

"Do not cross me, Genevieve," Valkryn snarls.

Her voice pierces the ringing in my ears.

"You have absolutely no idea what you're doing."

Get up! Genevieve, get up.

I roll onto my stomach. A drop of blood drips to the floor. I wipe the cut on my lip with the back of my hand, keeping my gaze locked on Valkryn.

"You seem worried." I cough as I raise myself.

Valkryn smirks. "You are an annoying girl, aren't you?" Her fists are radiating purple. "Do what you think you can."

My hands are still glowing. I cast them in her direction.

Craaaaaaack!

The beams radiate through the prison as they rush towards Valkryn. She raises her hands, forming a black shield that shatters my magic, scattering it into broken pieces.

"Try again!" she shrieks, and throws her own spells back at me.

Crap!

I raise my hands to my chest and pull them apart,

forming a light barrier. Her spells hit it and disappear, fading into the air as quickly as they formed.

She flicks her hands at the floor. The dark shadow appears beneath my feet again, but this time I jump out of the way.

As her spell bursts through the ground, I counter by casting my hands toward her several times. The beams shoot out and whiz across the hallway. Over and over and over and over.

She ends her casting to focus on deflecting mine. And I take off running.

What is going on?

What's happening?

What is happening!

My thoughts are uncontrollable, gnawing at me with an insatiable hunger. My world is blurred as I race forward, unsure of where to go. I am running. Breathing. I am alive.

But for how long?

None of this is making any sense. I have magical powers. I just used them. I saw them come from me. I am a paladin. I am being hunted.

I am wanted *dead*.

My breathing quickens. Chest tightens. Blood pounds through my body. Heart feels like it's going to explode.

Lub-dub! Lub-dub! Lub-dub! Lub-dub!

Genevieve. Look out!

The two guards from outside the prison are now in front of me.

"What's going on here? Stop!" one of them shouts, as I barrel towards them.

I shoot my hand out in front of me, and their bodies

are thrown through the air like ragdolls.

"Ahhhhh!" The first guard catapults across the vast room, and disappears into the distance.

Thud!

His screams halt.

"Wait! Wha—no!" The second guard slams against one of the nearby cell barriers.

His body writhes as the electricity courses through him.

I freeze in place, my mouth hanging open as I watch the smoke rise before he slumps to the ground.

Oh, my God. What have I done? What have I done!

Just go!

But I'm too late.

A shadowy wall towers into the air right in front of me as I'm about to take off. The shadows dance madly as they wind up to the ceiling, obscuring any chance of escape I could have.

I turn around and see Valkryn glaring at me with enraged eyes.

"I don't care what the Dark Lady wants. I will kill you myself," she hisses, through snarled lips.

I take a step back, my hands raised.

Ready to fight.

Crunnnnnnnnnch!

The ground around Valkryn rises, engulfing her legs in concrete until it reaches her waist. She stares down at her lower body, unable to move.

"What!" she screeches, waving her hands.

She pounds her fists against the solid material, but nothing happens.

Booooooooooooooooom!

The ground around her erupts in a thunderous

explosion. I fall to the floor as the earth shakes beneath my feet, cracking in several places. I cough and close my eyes as a cloud of dust penetrates the air.

When it clears, there is a crater where Valkryn had been frozen just moments before.

I crawl forward and peer over the edge. Far below, her body is sprawled and contorted, motionless as rubble continues to tumble into the pit on top of her.

"It's cute that the new little paladin thinks she can take on one of the most adept shadow Formulists known to this land. Almost laughable, ah?" Naxxorius morphs into focus on the other side of the crater. "Fortunately for you, I thought it would be in my best interest to help you out of that mess."

I stand, testing my balance.

"Well. What are you waiting for?" The elemental's voice echoes through the prison. "Do you want to go save your brother, or not?"

21

ESCAPE

PALADIN.

Freaking paladin!

My brain races past the rest of my body. My feet press against the hard floor, but I feel nothing. Nothing but the jarring truth crashing against my mind.

I am a paladin.

My mother enters my thoughts, and I can't help but smile at thinking about what she'd say.

Naxxorius flicks his wrist at Maldridge's cell. *Pop!* The barrier dissipates.

Scythe's body lies on the ground in a pool of dark, glistening blood.

"Ah," Naxxorius glides over the corpse. "Such a shame, really. Tied up in all this mess." He motions to Danny. "At least you got your brother back, yes?"

My brother. I feel a pang of selfishness clench my heart as I divert my attention from Scythe, and move into my brother's cell. He's lying on the cement slab, still in the same position I saw him when I first arrived in the Prison Ward, which now seems like centuries ago.

"Danny," I whisper.

I run over to him, throw myself onto his warm body, and run my fingers through his messy brown hair. He remains asleep, a serene look spread across his face.

"He will come around," Maldridge says, from behind. "Valkryn gave him something to sleep." He turns to Naxxorius. "Speaking of..."

"She won't be a problem. For now. But you know she doesn't stay down long."

"What about Scythe?" The words taste bitter on my tongue.

Maldridge glances at his body. "Genevieve." His eyes crease as he smiles at me, a warm glow radiating from his aged face. "Do you know what a paladin is?"

The confusion at his question must be apparent on my face, because he doesn't wait for a response.

"A holy warrior. Champion of light. Bringer of life. Genevieve, *you* are a paladin." He looks at Scythe's body. "You have the power to defeat death."

"I...what?"

He grabs my hand and guides me to the outside of Danny's cell. His touch is warm against my clammy skin.

"Kneel, Genevieve."

I hesitate, my gazed fixed on Scythe, just inches from my feet.

"It's okay." He helps me to the ground. "Now place your hands on his chest."

My hands tremble as I reach out and place my fingertips atop his bloodstained shirt. My heart races inside my throat as I push down against his chest. There is no warmth, no heartbeat. No life. His eyes are closed, and his face expressionless.

The thought flickers through my mind as to whether this serenity could be the most peace he has had in some time. With death, there is no pain, no suffering, no heartbreak. At its worst, there is nothing. And at its best?

"What am I doing?" I whisper.

"Your mother asked me the same question." Maldridge's words slice across my ears like a steel sword.

I feel my hands grow warm against Scythe's chest. A golden glow radiates from my palms, spreading across Scythe's body like a rippling wave. The dazzling sparks illuminate around us, and I squint as their intensity grows. The adrenaline rushes through my body. I feel my blood is on fire, coursing through my veins like gasoline.

"Come on," I hiss, through gritted teeth, my eyes stinging, my arms numb. "Come on!"

An explosion of white light, followed by the steady motion of a chest rising beneath my hands.

I open my eyes and look down. Scythe is staring back at me, with a weak smirk.

"Hey, Genevieve."

I open my mouth to speak, but can't find the words.

And then Scythe's lips are pressed against mine.

For the first time since we've met, the air around him is not chilled. His lips are not frostbitten. His skin not pale.

His warm kiss penetrates deep into my bones, as though I'm being caressed by sun-touched silk. I close my eyes, and I am surrounded by nothing but bliss.

"Truly an enchanting moment, yes?" Naxxorius coos, from nearby.

I open my eyes as Scythe pulls away.

"Are we finished now, ah?"

Scythe stands, pushing his hair back as he looks down at his bloodied shirt.

"What the hell happened?" He steps away from the pool of blood on the floor.

"I'm a paladin." I can't help but laugh. "And I just resurrected you."

Pretty sure he thinks I'm joking.

"Wait...but Valkryn?"

"Preoccupied at the moment," Naxxorius says. "And unless you're willing to deal with her soon, I would recommend we get moving."

"Genevieve!"

My heart stops when I hear Jensen's voice.

Seconds later, I'm wrapped in his embrace. I shift as he holds me, a deep pit rising in my stomach.

Jensen pulls away and looks around.

He spots the blood on the floor. "Whoa! What's going on?"

"Just asked the same thing," Scythe says.

I become panic-stricken as I watch the two of them lock gazes.

"You look like you've been better." Jensen points to Scythe's shirt.

"I could say the same about you. You get choked out, or what?"

"It's nothing." Jensen rubs the purple bruise across his neck. "Who defeated the shadow mage?"

"That would be Naxxorius's fine work," Maldridge says.

"Magister!" Jensen bows. "I'm glad to see you're okay."

"Thank you, Mister Saint Clair." Maldridge smiles back. "Let's get you out of here so I can say the same." He nods to Naxxorius, who conjures an access point.

"Jensen, go grab Genevieve's brother." Maldridge points to Scythe. "Please give the portal key to Genevieve. You're going to come with me."

"What? No way! I'm going back with Genevieve and—"

Maldridge holds up his hand. "There is no room for discussion here, Scythe. You are coming with me. Genevieve is in capable hands with Jensen. I'm sure you know this."

Scythe growls under his breath, grasping the key. He hesitates before reaching out to me.

"Here," he says.

My fingertips brush his warm hand as I grab the crystal.

"Thank you for your assistance, Naxxorius," Maldridge says. "I appreciate your help."

"You are one of the only people I charge no price for my services, Magister. But be warned, even I will have my limits eventually."

"Duly noted." Maldridge motions to Scythe. "Come along. We have a lot to do."

"Where are we going?"

"To my hometown, Nottingwood. Naxxorius. If you will, please."

"Wait!" Scythe says. "Genevieve."

I hold my breath.

"Be good."

With a flick of Naxxorius's wrist, Maldridge and Scythe disappear.

"Ready?" Naxxorius turns towards us.

"Yeah." Jensen returns from the cell, with Danny cradled in his arms. "Let's go."

I follow him over to the portal.

"Just pull the crystal apart," he says, "twist it, and close it again."

I hold my breath as I follow his instructions.

Naxxorius takes one final look around the Prison Ward before evaporating.

And then we're gone.

The Dark Lady stares down at Valkryn's crumpled body.

"They're gone, Voidress," an approaching guard says, in a defeated tone. "Mengurion Maldridge seems to have escaped as well."

Kingston stands beside the Dark Lady, his arms crossed. Silence paints the air.

The Prison Ward's door opens, and two more guards rush in.

"My Lady, it's true. The Magician is dead. And we found this."

Kingston becomes rigid as the guard hands the Dark Lady one of the Magician's inventions. She grabs it from him, watching the device emit white light as it whirls in her grasp.

"What is it?" Kingston says.

"Blaine's lantern," she replies. "It's supposed to tell you what kind of Formulist somebody is."

"So why's it spinning like that?"

"Because the last sample he put in here was from a paladin." The Dark Lady's voice scathes. "Get Valkryn out of this hole and clean up Fortrunner's lab." She pushes the lantern into Kingston's arms before turning to leave. "And make sure you kill the guards who let them escape, if they aren't already dead."

Her presence cloaks the Prison Ward in a ghastly chill, even after the door shuts behind her.

The rattle resonates through my teeth and into my skull as my feet slam down on the metal platform. It takes a moment for my clouded vision to focus, the bright stars and black dots slowly fading from my view, allowing the church's nave to morph into appearance.

Jensen stands next to me, with Danny still in his arms.

"Are you okay?" he says.

I nod. "Yeah, I think so."

An eerie quiet drapes the old church in a dampened shroud. I realize I'm no longer the same person that I was when I last left this church just hours before.

"I feel like we have a lot to talk about." I chuckle.

He sighs and stares down at the makeshift portal on the floor.

"I'm just glad you're okay." He shakes his head. "I don't even know what happened tonight."

"Yeah..."

"Let's get you two home." He nods down at Danny. "He'll wake up in the morning and won't remember anything."

As we near the church's exit, he turns around and outstretches his hand. A dazzling fireball illuminates the church's walls as it launches towards the Magician's portal. It explodes into a fiery inferno, the flames grasping at the nearby pews and licking across the aged wood.

"We can't run the risk of letting any part of his magic here survive." Jensen's voice is dark.

And as the church's shadows dance across his face, I see it washed in a forlorn expression.

After we lay Danny in the backseat of my car, and I get behind the wheel, I take one more look at the old church, engulfed in flames that burn against the midnight sky.

We just destroyed a church.

I've seen more fires and destruction in the last week than in my entire life.

What next?

I push the thought out of my mind and keep driving.

But really.

What next?

22

DEAL

THE YOUNG GUARD PUSHES OPEN the black steel doors. As their creak reverberates through the throne room, he inches forward onto the violet runner, gazing down its long distance to the wide-set stairs on either side of the Dark Lady's landing. He knows she sits atop the Void Throne, but from where he stands, he can only see shadows cast across the chamber from the multiple light fixtures that line the blackened walls. They illuminate an iridescent purple glow, creating the illusion of an amethyst fog rolling through the room.

His breath quickens as he approaches closer. He has not been in the throne room often, but the few times he has always causes a feeling of impending doom deep within his heart. Whether it's from the emptiness of the Gothic vaulted ceilings, or the haunting tension that hangs in the air, he does not know. The only awareness he senses is the uncertainty of how the Dark Lady will react to his presence.

He stops below the landing, unsure of how to proceed.

"My Lady." His voice echoes infinitely around the

room. "My Lady?" he repeats, after a few moments of no response.

His body tenses beneath his heavy armor.

The Dark Lady remains motionless on her throne. From where he stands, he sees her bodyguard, Vin'jork, towering at her side.

The metal throne's back rises high into the air, with each side tapering into an ornate swirl. Its arms jut forward, with decorative carvings of grasping claws wrapping around dazzling onyx crystals that root into the base of the throne.

"What is your name?" the Dark Lady finally says.

The bird skull adorning her head glares down at the young guard.

"James Parlington, my Lady. But...I go by Flagg."

"Flagg. You are a new trainee?"

"Yes, my Lady."

"And yet you're here talking to me?"

"I—"

She holds up her hand. "I don't want an excuse."

"Of course, my Lady."

"Tell me why you're here."

"There is a Visidium that wishes to speak with you. He was rather persistent that I let you know. I told him you probably wouldn't—"

"I said no excuses."

"Right...sor-sorry."

"Well, I suppose it doesn't matter now, does it? Whether or not I want to talk to the elemental, I have no choice."

"What?" Flagg says.

"Your Visidium is already here. Isn't that right, Naxxorius?"

"Ah, how did you know?" Naxxorius' melodic tone

rings out across the room.

Flagg feels the air stir next to him as the Visidium morphs into form.

"What other elemental would be foolish enough to enter the Void Keep?" The Dark Lady stands from her throne to glide over to the edge of her landing, and rests her hands against the silver balcony rail. "Although, I suppose any of you meaningless vapors could have tricked this guard to get you in here."

"Now, now. Don't blame poor Sir Parlington. He's merely doing his job, ah?" Naxxorius places his hand on Flagg's shoulder. "He's still learning."

"What do you want, plunderer?" the Dark Lady hisses. "I don't have time for your nonsense."

"No, you certainly don't, do you? I heard about your recent troubles. Valkryn Salharia defeated by a couple amateur Formulists? And the death of Blaine Fortrunner? *Tsk, tsk.* Things are certainly not looking good for the Voidweavers at the moment."

Vin'jork steps forward, hand on his sword's sheath.

"No need for violence, ah?" Naxxorius reaches into his cloak. "I came to make a proposition." He throws a cell phone at Vin'jork.

"What is this?" the Dark Lady says, as Vin'jork hands her the phone.

She takes the device in her gloved hand.

"That is Genevieve DeWinter's cell phone," Naxxorius replies. "I took it from her while she was in the Voidlands."

The Dark Lady rubs her fingers over the screen.

"I wanted you to see for yourself that I have made contact with the girl. I know she is important to you. And of course, I would be willing to obtain her."

"And your price?"

"Given that two of your commanders have already been bested by the girl, I must warn that my request is substantial."

The Dark Lady hands the phone back to Vin'jork.

"Axraxus needs to be returned to the Visidium. There is no reason for the Voidweavers to control the city, you know that. The Wastelands hold no value to your cause."

"I see," the Dark Lady says. "And is this your own suggestion? Or have you discussed it with the other elementals?"

"My own doing. They are not involved."

"Of course they aren't. I'm sure somewhere in those manipulative shadows of yours, this plan will only aid you in whatever ploy you're trying to pull off."

"There is no duplicity here. Except for the actions *you've* committed, Dark Lady."

"Careful, plunderer. Don't forget where you're standing."

"And don't forget where you're sitting."

The Dark Lady tightens her grasp on the balcony.

"How long have we known each other?" Naxxorius glides over to the stairs and ascends towards the landing.

Vin'jork goes to draw his sword once more, but the Dark Lady signals him to stand down.

"Ten years? Fifteen? Twenty? Time just seems to fall away eventually." Naxxorius reaches the top of the stairs, floating inches from the Dark Lady. "Must I remind you that you are here because of me, *Dark Lady?*" He motions to the skull atop her head. "You owe me."

The Dark Lady's lips are taut against her pale skin.

"You bring me Genevieve DeWinter, and Axraxus

is yours." She places her hand against Naxxorius's silver cloak. "But know that if I see you again before you have the girl, I will kill you. And then I will kill every other repulsive elemental that wanders this forsaken land."

The echo of the steel doors slices through the tension as several guards erupt into the throne room.

"Voidress!" One of the guards pants as he bounds towards the throne. "My Lady, we are being attacked."

The Dark Lady and Naxxorius turn toward the guards.

"Outside! At the Cathedral."

Naxxorius snickers. "Well, this certainly isn't going the way you planned, ah?" He disappears before she can respond.

"Shall I go?" Vin'jork says.

The Dark Lady shakes her head and descends the stairs.

"The recent incompetency is just baffling to me. I'll deal with this myself."

Flagg Parlington breathes a sigh of relief as the Dark Lady exits the throne room, knowing that at any moment he could have been the next target of her wrath.

23

REVELATION

THE DARK LADY STEPS INTO THE COURT OF ANGUISH.

The air is thick with black fog, and echoes with the sound of explosions. Before her, countless Voidweavers are strewn across the area, battling with the Void Keep's invaders.

She descends the colossal stone stairs as her hands swirl with magic. A mixture of golden light and black hues lace through her fingers, building itself into a larger sphere. When she reaches the cobblestone ground, she pauses to scan the area.

And then she throws her hands out in front of her.

Several groups of soldiers explode as her dark magic bombards them from all directions. Their screams rip through the air as their mangled bodies are catapulted across the courtyard, leaving only remnants of human flesh.

Her magic cracks through the sky like lightning hitting a tree as she targets more groups, sauntering across the grounds as she unleashes her wrath.

Flagg Parlington emerges from the Void Keep and stands at the top of the entrance, where the Dark Lady had been just minutes before. His eyes are wide with fear as he watches her execute the fighters, killing not only the invaders, but her own Voidweavers.

The sky flashes with a myriad of colors, the result of various Formulists casting their magic during the ensuing battle. Harsh, metallic clangs reverberate through Flagg's ears as combatants wage war with their own deadly weapons. The invading soldiers are clad in silver armor, a stark contrast to the onyx-black material the Voidweavers wear.

Flagg watches as the Dark Lady's slaughter continues through the battleground, clearing a path towards the cathedral. The building's spires pierce high into the darkened sky, adding a foreboding shadow that drapes the distant earth.

The ground beneath Flagg shakes.

"Airships approaching!"

A booming horn bellows through the air as several monstrous machines rise from the edge of the land's abyss like a waking behemoth. Flagg's attention shifts from the Dark Lady to the massive artillery ships that are now churning through the air, obscuring any remaining light that still had the courage to illuminate this lifeless land. Their gargantuan wings jut out from each side, attached to large propellers that whirl, roaring out their deafening hum. The silver engines on the back of the steel ships leave behind contrails, marking the paths they've taken like an intricate treasure map.

Flagg takes a deep breath and runs into battle. As he draws his sword from its sheath, he spots Kingston Starmantle fighting a group of invading soldiers, several yards away. He rushes over, his face drenched with sweat beneath his helmet, and his heart pounding, intensifying with every step he takes.

Kingston swings his sword and executes the last soldier as Flagg arrives.

"What are you doing?" Kingston watches Flagg stand frozen in place.

His hands are clenched around his sword's hilt, but his body refuses to move.

"Don't just stand there! You need to—"

Whoosh!

Flagg jolts to life as Kingston crashes into the ground, spewing dirt and rubble into the air as he slides several feet before stopping. A soldier looms in front of him, his silver gauntlet outstretched and frosted with ice from the spell he just released.

"Ugh," Kingston gasps, using his sword to steady himself to his knees.

The immense figure's silver armor clangs as he lumbers towards him.

Flagg raises his sword and charges. The soldier turns his head to see Flagg, and brings up his hand. A blast of ice explodes from it in a shattered cacophony, and crashes into Flagg. His sword drops as he's catapulted back across the court, and he slams against the stairs, knocking him unconscious.

The soldier looks back down at Kingston. "Get up."

Kingston stays kneeling.

"Starmantle, *get up.*"

Kingston glares at the silver helmet, which is shaped like an owl's head. He's barely able to make out the eyes behind.

"I. Said. Get. Up!" The soldier swings his sword at Kingston.

Screeeeeeeeech!

Vin'jork's sword blocks the soldier's attack, and

the soldier stumbles backward. Vin'jork looks down at Kingston, who sees his own face reflected in the bull's horns of the black helmet.

"Go to the Cathedral." Vin'jork turns back to face the soldier. "And leave me be."

Kingston nods as he returns to his feet. He gives each soldier a onceover before disappearing into the waves of battle.

"I thought I'd be able to draw you out." The silver soldier points his sword at Vin'jork. "But I didn't think it was going to be *that* easy."

"Hello, Rok'jin. It's been a long time." Vin'jork stands his ground. "If you came here hoping to make amends, I have no interest in doing so. Brother or not, I will kill you if necessary."

"Well, then." Rok'jin flashes a pearlescent smile as he gets into a battle stance. "Shall we begin?"

The Dark Lady reaches the cathedral and pushes open the black steel doors. Inside, the walls are lined with century-old torches, their orange flames glistening off the dusty marble floor. Chandeliers bathed in spider webs hang down the center aisle, equally spaced and running all the way to the altar. Although once majestic Baroque fixtures, only candles burnt down to waxy nubs remain.

As the Darky Lady proceeds, the arching ceilings twist high above, their inlays decorated with peeling designs unrecognizable after centuries of wear.

On the altar's stairs stands a man.

"I feel as though it were just yesterday I set foot in here." The man's powerful voice fills every corner of the cathedral. "Time's a funny thing."

"To me it feels like a thousand lifetimes ago." The Dark Lady's words are hollow. She stops several feet from the man. "Lifetimes of imprisonment."

He stands rigid, facing her. His bright blue eyes are the only warmth radiating within the cathedral, and the kindness in his face seems at odds with the layers of armor that encase his body. His short silver hair blows ever so slightly with the wisps of wind that manage to sneak into the sanctuary.

"Look at you." He lifts his head as he scans the Dark Lady's features.

A thin beam of light from the ceiling's cracks illuminates the side of his face, displaying his sharp nose and prominent jaw. He places his gauntlet-cladded hand over his mouth and chin as his eyes fill with sorrow.

"What have you become?"

"Do not pity me, Dorndrick," the Dark Lady spews. "Do not pretend that you care. My existence is the result of your betrayal, your failure to see the world as it justly is."

"Your existence?" Dorndrick steps down from the altar. "*Your* existence? No, you misunderstand. I have no pity for *you*. But pity for what you have done. You stand here now in front of me as the Dark Lady, a creation from your own warped mind, driven to even further madness over the last ten years. Devoid of your true power, and slowly destroying the only thing left of Addisyn DeWinter." Dorndrick scowls. "She should have just killed you."

"But she couldn't. And do you know why?" The Dark Lady gleams. "Because she was weak. She believed that morality existed, that all people were inherently good." She scoffs. "There is nothing in the world that matters but power. Our entire existence is one person trying to get ahead of another. Whether it is eye for eye, or scheme by scheme, the measure of a man equates to his final status of dominance, not good deeds."

"You didn't always believe that," Dorndrick says. "When I first met you—before the Dark Lady, before the Void King, before Gresalmur's corruption—you shared Addisyn's sentiment. I chose to mentor you for the good I saw, for the paladin I knew you could become." He shakes his head. "It is my fault that you were lost. I blame no one but myself for that failure."

"And therein lies your weakness, Dorndrick Wolfshire. Where did your moral compass get you but misery and pain?"

"I know what you're doing. I know about the Binding Spell. You think there's a chance you can return to your former body if you find Addisyn's daughter? Well, we won't let you. The Abolishment has taken arms once more, and we will watch you fail again."

"Silence!" The Dark Lady's shriek sheers past Dorndrick's ears, and her body emits a shadowy glow as she rises into the air. "The Abolishment is nothing. Addisyn DeWinter is nothing. *You* are nothing." Her eyes burn vibrant amethyst from behind the bird skull that adorns her head. "All that I am, all that I have built, all that I have accomplished within the last decade has been with my own identity. My own will, my own autonomy, my own control. Banewind speaks of me in whispers, for fear that I might at any moment destroy what precious life it has left. The Voidweavers return to take back what has always been ours, what has never belonged to anyone—to break the chains of order and structure, the false promise of *freedom*. The world will be born again from the throes of chaos, and life will be created as intended. The Binding Spell may have trapped me within Addisyn DeWinter's body, but I can assure you that I, the Void King, am still very much alive. And I will be the one to triumph in a glorious return."

A pillar of shadow erupts from her hands and hurls towards Dorndrick, just barely missing him as he rolls to the side. It crashes into the altar and ricochets, knocking one of the chandeliers from its chain. The light fixture clamors to the floor, shattering mere inches from Dorndrick's legs.

Bright light bursts from his hands as he counters her attack. The Dark Lady nimbly spins to the side and sends out another barrage of shadows, painting the marble floor in dark, bubbling gloom. Dorndrick jumps to his feet and runs as he draws his sword from its sheath. He leaps high and strikes down with a mighty thrust.

The Dark Lady disappears as his sword lashes through the empty air, slamming into the floor with a deafening clang. He pivots around just in time to block the black shadow orb rushing toward him. With a swing of his sword, it explodes backwards and crashes into the Dark Lady, jarring the bird skull from her head, which clatters to the ground with a hollow echo that dissipates across the cathedral.

The Dark Lady's cloak rustles as she drops back to the ground.

"I will break the Binding Spell, Dorndrick. And when I do, I will return to my body, and Addisyn will return to hers. And then I will kill her. And then I will kill you. And along the way, I will destroy everything that Banewind has ever come to know."

"It must drive you mad to wake every morning and know you're still a prisoner." Dorndrick pants between words. "The once almighty Void King, trapped in his vanquisher's body." He stares into the face of Genevieve's mother. "While somewhere out there, Addisyn DeWinter possesses yours, locked away in slumber. A constant reminder of your failure."

The Dark Lady glares back, an amethyst glow still surrounding her blue eyes. Her blonde hair lays disheveled across her pale face. She walks over to the skull and picks it up in her gloved hand.

"You are here, no doubt, because you came in search of Felyx's relic." She positions the skull back on her head, once again hiding the features of Addisyn DeWinter. "Foolish of you to think I would leave it exposed."

"I knew it would no longer be here the moment I learned you murdered him." Dorndrick's stoic expression morphs into a sardonic grin. "But after ten years, I wanted you to see I was still here, waiting, ready to raise arms once again. Until my dying breath, I will never allow you to return to your former self."

"At one time, when you were my mentor, I would have found your bravery and tenacity something to admire." The Dark Lady faces Dorndrick. "But now I see nothing but a frail fool."

Kingston throws open the cathedral doors just as the Dark Lady's magic tangles around Dorndrick. The dark tendrils grasp his armor, paralyzing him as she raises his body high into the air.

"Lamentable. Fragile. Worthless." The Dark Lady's voice resonates, each word dancing through the air like a demonic spell. "You are *nothing*. And you will always be nothing."

Kingston stands helplessly in the middle of the aisle, his gaze fixated on the Dark Lady's magic spilling out around her like a black steam billow. Dorndrick's screams rip through Kingston's ears, tying his stomach into a tighter knot with each intensifying cry.

"Yes. Feel the pain. The unmatched power of my spells. Let it consume you to the point of insanity. Yield to its command."

"You...cannot...win," Dorndrick roars, through gritted teeth. "I...will...never...yield...to...you!"

"Foolish paladin. Then you will die!"

The ground beneath Kingston's feet starts to rumble. Rubble and dust fall from the ceiling, hitting the nearby pew. He raises his gaze and sees the cathedral's rafters shaking. The doors burst open once more, and several Voidweaver soldiers rush in.

"Drago'kkoa!" one of them yells, his hysterical screams breaking through Dorndrick's cries. "Dark Lady, Drago—"

The cathedral's roof rips apart in a thunderous blast, the deafening sound nearly shattering Kingston's body as he's thrown to the floor by the sheer magnitude of the attack. The cathedral's structure crumbles apart like brittle clay, spewing its contents to the ground in a shower of falling projectiles. Kingston's eyes widen with fear as a large stone comes flailing down in his direction, giving him just mere seconds to roll to the side to avoid being crushed by the immense structure. The guards behind him leap into the nearest pew, clamoring underneath it to obtain any protection they can get.

A bloodcurdling, monstrous roar penetrates the night sky. Kingston stands petrified as a gigantic, shimmering claw rises high behind the cathedral's back wall, like a zombie's hand emerging from the grave. The sharp talons slam down into the stone, causing more of the foundation to crumble as the creature lifts itself into the cathedral. A massive reptilian head emerges from the night's shadows as another claw grasps onto the other side of the wall. Its long neck protrudes into the cathedral, so enormous that not any other part of its body can be seen.

The creature looks down at the Dark Lady, who is still standing with Dorndrick strewn in the air. It raises its lips into a ferocious snarl and flashes its dagger-sharp teeth as it lets out another thunderous roar. Its belly destroys the final part of the cathedral's wall as it moves forward, smashing its leg onto the altar and bringing with it an avalanche of rubble that stops inches from the Dark Lady.

Kingston gawks at the dragon in utter disbelief. Its body shadows the entirety of the ground, pulling everyone into darkness. Along its head, neck, body, and tail is silver armor that matches the set Dorndrick wears, casting the moon's glow back into the sky as though it were a light's beacon.

It lowers its head down toward the Dark Lady. She pulls her hand away from Dorndrick, who falls to the ground like discarded trash. The Dark Lady stands unyielding as the creature's glowing white eyes dazzle at her. Its breath can be seen rising into the night's sky, now adorning the cathedral. She moves closer to the beast and stretches out her hand as it brings its own head closer to her.

"Even now, she hasn't forgotten you," Dorndrick says, weak but confident.

He is ascending the armor on one of the creature's legs.

The creature retracts its head high into the air. It lets out another decimating howl before exhaling a beam of stunning white light that shoots into the night like a fiery comet. Its wings jut out, revealing the veiny transparent undersides as they begin to flap violently, raising the creature into the air.

Dorndrick casts his gaze at the Dark Lady one last time.

"Away!" He grabs the metal bar that rests across the dragon's back.

As he settles into position, the beast delivers one final roar before disappearing into the twilit night.

Kingston inches towards the wrecked altar, along with the shaken soldiers following him. He stops several feet from the Dark Lady.

She continues to stare up into the night.

Kingston hears footsteps and turns to see Vin'jork stepping through the cathedral's rubble. The soldier passes Kingston without acknowledgement, and halts next to the Dark Lady. She stands motionless for several moments.

"Go," she murmurs.

Vin'jork nods.

Kingston waits a moment before turning away.

The Dark Lady stares on as she watches the last of the airships disappear into the distance.

24

FUTURE PLANS

To the Esteemed Members of the Council of the Formulists:

I, Mengurion Maldridge, Former 56th Magister of the Council of the Formulists, do hereby attest that the following information is factual, objective, and true in its utmost entirety.

As you are well-aware, I was held hostage by the Voidweavers for a period of four weeks. During my captivity, I spent almost all of my time confined to a prison cell, in isolation and withdrawn from the outside world. I was, however, able to learn a fair amount of information from the whispers of guards and the few run-ins I had with various members of the Voidweavers. It is with a grave and heavy heart that, with undoubted certainty, I can confirm that they have returned to full operation to resurrect their former leader, Ganstin Remores, known by many different names, but most colloquially as the Void King. And at the current moment, he is alive.

The Voidweavers' current leadership is in the hands of a woman. Referred to as the Dark Lady, she is actually the Void King inhabiting the body of Addisyn DeWinter, and is the igniting force that has now driven the Voidweavers back into existence across the lands of Banewind. At the time, it appears that the group is still in its infancy, but has been functioning in the shadows for the better part of the last decade. I do not know what is to come of their emergence, but there should be no doubt that this could lead to catastrophic ends if not properly dealt with immediately.

To make matters more complicated, there is a young woman, Genevieve DeWinter, the daughter of our beloved and heroic past Holy Guardian, Addisyn DeWinter, who I can verify by first-account witness, has the Paladin's blood coursing through her veins. As I write this letter, one of our top priorities should be the safety of the girl. The Voidweavers seek to capture her as a means of breaking the Binding Spell that Addisyn DeWinter used to lock away the Void King's body, thereby weakening him substantially by separating him from his physical form. The consequence of this forced Addisyn DeWinter to become imprisoned in the Void King's body when they switched forms. But she was aware of what was happening and chose to do so in order to protect Banewind.

I fear that if they are able to succeed in her daughter's capture, we will be doomed to suffer the same brutality of the Voidweavers' wrath once more, as the Void King would be restored to his full power and form. Make no mistake, history has shown that there is always more blood to be spilled...a world to be asphyxiated as before.

Miss DeWinter has already made allies with multiple Formulists, and it is with good faith that I can confidently say the St. Clair Family has volunteered to keep the girl safe. I have already spoken with Gerard St. Clair, Co-Chancellor on the Council of the Formulists, who has graciously agreed to personally watch over the girl for the next several months. Of course, given the complexity of this situation, details are still being worked out, which is why I write this letter to you.

I ask that a meeting of the Council of the Formulists takes place with Mr. St. Clair to create a detailed plan to alleviate the acute issues brought before us. Unfortunately, I am indisposed at the time, dealing with another thread unraveling from this tapestry, and I will not be returning to Quam'Naldon any time soon to reconvene with the Council. As such, please consider this letter a formal legal decree, and follow through with the appropriate accommodations.

I will be in touch as soon as possible. Until then, all my best, and keep alert with wary eyes.

Warm regards,

Mengurion Wilmott Maldridge
Former 56th Magister of the
Council of the Formulists

Jensen folds the letter in half once he finishes reading, and runs his fingers across the crease multiple times as the words turn over in his head. He finally hands it over to Sadie, who is sitting next to him on the couch in her living room.

"As you can see, Maldridge insults the Council with his scathing words, making us appear inept, as though we're merely sitting around twiddling our thumbs." The man across from Jensen scoffs.

As he shifts in his chair, the material of his golden cloak ruffles beneath him, like waterfalls tumbling to the floor. He sits erect, with his hands positioned on his knees, as though he is ready to jump up at any moment.

"I think you're misinterpreting the letter's intent, Thaddeus," another man says, in a gentle voice.

He sits next to Thaddeus in a matching chair, but with a much calmer demeanor. He is wearing a charcoal gray suit, with his hands folded in his lap. The ceiling's light reflects off his newly shined black shoes.

"Personally, I don't find any ill-will in Magister Maldridge's letter. What I *do* see, quite obviously, is a real fear for what has already transpired."

"*Ex*-Magister, Gerard," Thaddeus says, through gritted teeth. "Don't let that senile old fool trick you into thinking he has real power anymore. The man is frail and weak. He was removed from the position for good reason. And in my opinion, I see this as just a pathetic attempt at acting out for attention. He's desperate to relive his glory days and embarrass me along the way."

"With all due respect, Magister Loring," Sadie says, once she finishes reading the letter. "I politely disagree. I have known Mengurion Maldridge for almost my entire life, as have many, and there isn't a malicious bone in his body. He is in no way trying to undermine your authority. And as Gerard has already said, his concerns are legitimate, especially if the Void King is already here in the form of Addisyn DeWinter, or the Dark Lady, or whatever you want to refer to him as."

"Did you not listen to anything I said over the last hour?" Jensen says. "What more evidence could you possibly need?"

"Jensen," Gerard says, in a stern tone.

"Sorry, Dad, but it's true." Jensen throws himself back into the couch and folds his arms across his chest. "You guys weren't there for any of it."

"Yes, another dubious point that your son raises." Thaddeus rubs his silver goatee and turns to a woman in a red dress, standing next to him. "Trixie, you have transcribed all of Mister Saint Clair's extravagant tale, have you not?"

"Every word, Magister." The woman wears a Cheshire grin.

The fire-hydrant red lipstick and matching red curly hair that sits piled on top of her head is a stark contrast to her snow-white complexion. In front of her sits an antique typewriter, balanced on a slim, high-top table. She stands behind it, poised, with her red high heels pressing deep into the oriental rug that adorns Sadie's floor. As her fingers nimbly pound the keys, the constant *click-clack* echoes around the room. When she presses the button to reset the machine, the letters on the page peel off and float into the air, disappearing like tiny sparks as the page becomes blank once more.

"It is quite the tale, indeed," she says.

"It's not a tale. It's the truth," Jensen growls, starting to rise from the couch.

Sadie presses her hand to his shoulder. He catches her gaze as she shakes her head, and sighs deeply before relaxing back down on the cushion.

"Know that I say these things not to give you a hard time, or to belittle what you report. But rather, it is because this is my rightful duty as Magister. I need to make sure that the Council is armed with the appropriate—and unbiased—information. Why, we don't need to incite a civilian riot for no good reason, do we?" Thaddeus places his fingertips together in front of his pale face and furrows his brow. "No." He sighs, shaking his head. "We wouldn't want that."

"I understand where you're coming from, I do," Gerard says. "But Thaddeus, you have to admit that these reports are concerning. And while you might not have completed an official investigation on it, precautions should still be taken." He pauses, waiting for Thaddeus to reply, but nothing is said. "So as Maldridge alluded to in his letter, I have agreed to work on keeping Miss DeWinter safe— separate from my Council duties—and with the intention of not letting it interfere with my normal workflow." He gestures to Sadie. "Sadie has already been helping with the girl these last few weeks, and she has agreed to continue to do so. My family as well is willing to lend a hand in whatever way they can. I can assure you, it will not take any of the Council's time if you agree to this."

"What you tell me has no bearing on whether or not I agree to something, Gerard," says Thaddeus. "*I* am the Magister. And although I might hear your opinion or listen to your suggestions, the ultimate say is mine entirely. Do I make myself clear?"

"Now, now. There's no need to raise your voice," Gerard says. "I respect your leadership position, but let's not forget this is still a democracy, Thaddeus. The Council, I'm sure, would love to have an input on this subject as well. And if you don't approach them on this as a serious inquiry...well, I might just have to file a grievance against you." His lips curl into a faint smile. "And I'm sure that's something you'd rather avoid, am I correct?"

Thaddeus's face burns red. "Are you threatening me, Chancellor Saint Clair?"

"I'm sorry if that's how you interpret it."

Silence dances through the room.

Thaddeus stands. "I will look into this. But as I am sure you are aware, the Council has already listened to the tales woven by your son and Miss Hawthorne. It is highly doubtful their feelings will have changed. That being said, you may do what you will for the time being, with the caveat that you do not waste Formulist resources, or have it interfere with your routine work." He turns to Jensen. "My son, Thomas Loring, I'm sure you're aware, is head of administration at the Formulists' Institution of Academia and Educational Pursuit. He will no doubt want to meet Miss DeWinter. Especially if she claims to be what you say.

I will arrange for this to happen in the near future. Will that be an issue?"

"I—"

"No, not at all." Gerard remains focused on Thaddeus as he rises from his chair and holds out his hand. "Thank you, Magister. I truly appreciate you taking the time to consider this and meet with us."

Thaddeus wavers before clasping Gerard's hand.

"As I said, I do care for the safety of my people." Thaddeus briefly shakes his hand before pulling away. "I'll be in touch." He turns to Trixie and nods. "Miss LeRoux?"

"Ready, Magister." She taps on the typewriter.

The high-top table jumps to life and folds in on itself multiple times, engulfing the machine as it morphs into a slim briefcase. It hovers in the air until Trixie grabs its handle.

Sadie guides them up the staircase.

"Oh, and Gerard?" Thaddeus calls, once he reaches the second floor.

His silver ponytail slashes through the air as he turns his head around to glare down at Gerard and Jensen, who are standing in the living room.

"I'll be waiting for you to screw up."

They disappear into the hallway's darkness.

"What an idiot." Jensen plops back down onto the couch.

"A common theme among people in power." Gerard strolls over to the whiskey decanter and pours a drink. "You get used to it."

"You believe me, right?" Jensen says. "About everything that happened? With Valkryn and the Void Keep and all that?"

"Of course I do." Gerard's brown eyes crease as he smiles at Jensen. "Even if Mengurion Maldridge hadn't corroborated what you said, you've never been one to lie to me. Now on the other hand, your siblings..." He laughs, then takes a sip of whiskey and sighs. "I don't like this, though. It's all very...unsettling."

"They're gone," Sadie calls down, as she begins to descend the stairs.

"Sure they're not hanging back to spy on us?" Jensen moans.

"I watched them disappear through the portal myself. Almost had half a mind to shove them." Sadie sighs. "I don't like this."

"That's what Dad just said."

"Yeah, well, Thaddeus Loring is perhaps going to go down in history as the worst Magister yet." She shakes her head. "I don't understand politics. Who in his or her right mind would give that man authority?"

"Ignoramuses." Gerard rubs the side of his graying brown hair before resting his chin on his fist. "But we don't have the luxury of ethical considerations at the moment."

"So...what's the plan?" Jensen says.

"The plan is to do exactly as we said." Gerard takes another sip of his drink. "Keep Genevieve safe."

"And how are we supposed to do that when she's living at home with her family?"

"Leave that to me, Jensen." Sadie glances at Gerard. "I've already discussed this with your father. She'll reside here in my home, with me."

Jensen frowns.

"And you, of course."

"And the rest of the Saint Clair family," Gerard says.

"Huh?"

"Your mother can keep tabs on things at the Academy, and I'm going to send your siblings to come help out."

Jensen starts to speak.

"And before you object, this is nothing against you. Trust me, I am very grateful for what you and Sadie have already done. And a fine job it's been. But we are moving into territory that is extremely dangerous. This is something that is not to be handled on an individual basis."

"But—"

"Don't worry." Sadie smiles. "There's plenty of room for everybody here. It'll be fine."

"That's it?" Jensen says. "That's the plan?"

Gerard shakes his head. "No. Obviously not. There are going to be a lot of moving parts to this. Genevieve will need proper training as a paladin, which is going to be another issue in itself. But I'm working on those details. And of course, there is the matter of the Voidweavers' threat of doom."

"That isn't funny, Dad." Jensen groans.

"I don't mean it to be. I'm sure it will surprise you not the least to hear me say I have very little faith in the Council's aid at the moment. Which means our city, and world, is going to be vulnerable. So further strings will need to be pulled."

"You just heard Magister Loring," Jensen says. "He sounds less than enthused to help out."

"And that's fine. Really, it's better."

"Yeah, okay. And what if he finds out? I mean, I don't really trust the guy. Who knows what he'll do if you disobey him."

Gerard laughs. "Jensen, in my fifty-eight years of life,

I can assure you I have come across many worse individuals than Thaddeus Loring. He is the epitome of all bark and no bite. You learn how to...hmm, what am I trying to say? You learn how to properly muzzle those types of people, as necessary."

Jensen lets the conversation turn over in his mind, nodding as he runs through it again and again.

"Okay," he says. "Okay, yeah. This sounds good. What about Magister Maldridge? Do you know where he is right now?"

"Vaguely," Gerard says. "Again, it's just another level of complexity to this situation."

"Is he still with Scythe?" Jensen says.

"Yes."

Jensen waits. "And?"

"And nothing. That's all you need to know."

Jensen sighs. "I don't understand the secrecy. First off, you tell us not to mention Scythe to anyone, including the Council. So why? And secondly, if we are all supposed to be working together, how does keeping anything hidden possibly make any sense?"

"I understand what you're saying. And I agree. However, we have to wait for Maldridge and Scythe to finish doing what they're doing before we give any more details. It's just the way it is."

Jensen turns to Sadie. "Do you know what he's talking about?"

She pats his hand. "Your father is right. This isn't the priority that *you* need to worry about, so just do your best to go with it, okay? I know that's hard."

Jensen sighs. "I'm going to lie down."

"Good idea. We should all get some rest." Gerard places his empty cup back on the tray. "I'll be in touch shortly, Sadie. Will you be ready for us by the end of next week?"

"Yes, of course."

"Perfect." Gerard's face radiates the warmth and confidence he always projects. "This will work. Everything is going to be okay."

Jensen can't help but notice his father isn't looking them in the eyes as he speaks.

25

LABOR DAY

I DON'T KNOW WHAT'S BECOME OF MY LIFE.

Almost two weeks ago, I was getting ready to start my senior year of high school, trying to figure out the whole college application process, deciding where I wanted my life to go. I was fighting with my brother over who had to load the dirty dishes in the dishwasher, and unload the clean ones. I was enjoying the last summer I would have with my best friend before the first of our adult life started to unfold.

And now?

I've kissed a boy.

Kissed *two* boys.

Watched one of them die before my eyes.

Brought him back to life.

Been to another world, threatened by death, discovered I have magical powers, and learned my mother could still be alive...

No, I don't know what's become of my life.

And I'm not sure where it's going.

The night we get back from the Void Keep, by some divine intervention, my father is still out working late at the university. So Danny and I make it home without any issues. As everyone had assured me, he awakes the next morning with no recollection of the past day's events.

When I go to sleep, I dream once more about my Prince Charming. I stand at the top of the stairs, the white ballgown flowing around me. And again the lights dim, thunder roars, and I'm trapped, with nothing surrounding me but darkness.

This time, though, the man in the mask heads up the stairs towards me. I stand there grasping the rails, watching him approach. He's holding a hammer now, the same one I saw my mother wielding in the scrying bowl visions at the mall. He extends his hands, offering it to me. I grab it with my pearlescent-laced gloves, and a beam of light shoots into the sky, fracturing the blackened clouds. He removes his mask, but I can't see his face from the intensity of the white light. The air stills briefly, and then there's an explosion.

I jolt awake and push the dream out of my head, something I've gotten better at doing. To save face and avoid any suspicion, I manage to drag myself to school for the rest of the week. The days are unproductive, and I don't remember much, if anything, of what is taught. But Jensen and I spend our free time catching Katie up on what transpired, and talking with Sadie about possible plans and directions we can take.

"Can I see your powers?" Katie says, when she hears about my paladin abilities. "Oh, Jeannie, this is incredible!"

"I don't even know how to use them." I sigh.

Since the night in the Void Keep, they haven't come back. And I've tried a few times.

"They'll come eventually," Jensen says. "You just have to get proper training."

"Yeah, well, that's going to have to happen soon if we plan on rescuing my mother."

"I also hope Scythe is okay," Katie says. "I feel bad we didn't trust him sooner, but..." She sighs. "He's been through so much."

"I agree," Jensen says. "I'm already trying to think of what to say for an apology when I see him next."

"*If* you see him again," I say. "We don't even know where he is right now."

The weekend arrives, and I spend the majority of time with Dad, preparing for the party we're having on Labor Day. I sit and tell him about what's going on with the Formulists and Banewind, but leave out a significant number of details of my recent journeys so he won't worry too much. I feel okay with him knowing, but don't think it needs to go any further than that. As Jensen says, it's risky for others if they find out what's going on. I don't need to put any more people in harm's way than are already there.

"You sure someone's bringing more ice, Jeannie?" my dad says, from the backyard porch.

It's already Labor Day afternoon, and we're working tirelessly to get things ready.

The sound of ice being dumped into a cooler ricochets past my ears.

"This hardly seems to be enough," he says.

"Yes, stop worrying about it. The Millers are on top of it. Katie has already texted me." I look down at my new phone, then put it back into my pocket.

"Perfect." He pulls open the screen door, crumpling the wet plastic bags as he enters the family room. "That should just about do it. Everything's all set up. Daniel, did you clean the bathroom?"

"Mhm," my brother says.

He and Nick are sitting on the couch, pounding on their video game controllers.

"Hmm. I better check myself." Dad opens the freezer drawer and grabs several containers of hamburger patties. "But first, I'll get these defrosting."

"And I'm gonna go get ready." I turn to walk out of the kitchen, and my stomach ties into knots at the thought of Jensen meeting my dad.

He hadn't remembered him from the funeral, though.

"Let me know if you need anything else." I head up the stairs.

As I reach out to turn my bedroom's door handle, I freeze.

A red glow illuminates from under the door, casting across the white carpet. A shiver runs down my spine as I recall the night I saw the same iridescent light back in the mall.

The goosebumps spread as I crack open the door.

I step into my room, the usually bright atmosphere now starkly contrasted by the shadows and red hues that wrap through the air. There's a tingling sensation on the back of my neck as I close the door behind me.

"What are you doing here?" I whisper.

Ilona hovers at the opposite end of the room. Her maroon cloak quivers against the ground. A black veil still covers her face, staring back at me like a void.

"Genevieve." Her melodic voice echoes through the room. "Much has changed since last we met."

"I don't understand." I shake my head, "Why are you here? *How* are you here?"

"The Blazing Vision." She points to my desk drawer. "I gave the talisman to you. And with it, part of me remains. I am here because we need to talk."

I let the silence linger.

"I am here because I believe we can save your mother."

The little composure I've maintained falters, and the familiar burning sensation fills my eyes.

"What..."

"You've unlocked the truth. Your abilities as a paladin are hidden no more. And I believe that's enough to bring her back."

"How?"

"Find Ira of the Jintüroo. She'll know what to do."

"What are you talking about? Who is that?"

"I cannot stay long. The magic grows weak."

"Ilona!" I rush toward her.

As I approach, my legs become heavy, preventing me from moving, as though they were stuck in mud.

"Ira."

"And what about Isaac Banewind?" I say, remembering the last words spoken by Felyx Crimsley. "Am I supposed to find him, too?"

It's hard to tell, but I think her head tilts ever so slightly to the side.

Ding-dong, ding-dong, ding-dong.

The doorbell's high-pitched charm fractures me back to reality.

"Ilona, please. How do I get to my mother?"

She remains frozen, her black-gloved hands hanging at her sides.

"Jeannie!" my father calls. "Someone's at the door."

"One second." My gaze stays fixed on the Formulist.

"Please, Ilona—"

"Jeannie!"

"I said hold on!" I turn my head towards the door. When I look back, Ilona's gone.

Several minutes later, I head downstairs.

But I don't understand. Ilona seemed different this time. There was a sense of urgency in her voice, concern that had not been there when we first met. It was as though her confidence had been shaken, like something frightened her.

Yeah, something changed. But what?

Never mind, Genevieve. This isn't the time. I enter the kitchen. *Oh, crap!*

Now I know who was at the door so early. Jensen is sitting on the stool by the kitchen counter, wearing a broad grin. I hear my dad's loud laugh tumble through the air.

Katie walks in from the family room as she cracks open a can of soda, and waves when she sees me.

Jensen and my father turn to me.

"Jeannie!" My dad takes a swig of his beer. "Glad you finally decided to join us."

"Sorry. I was having a hard time finding what I wanted to wear..." I look from my dad to Jensen, and back again.

Scythe's kiss penetrates my mind, but I dissipate the image.

"So I see you've met."

"You didn't get the door." Katie laughs, taking a seat at the kitchen table. "Jensen wanted to come early to meet your dad, so I gave him a ride." She looks at my father. "My parents are coming with ice later."

"That's fine, Katie. Perfect." His voice light and warm. "And I have to say, Genevieve, I like this new friend of yours so far. He has a strong handshake."

"Oh, well, thank goodness for that," I mutter.

Jensen laughs.

"Why don't you all head outside?" Dad pulls open the oven. "I'll start to get things ready before the other guests arrive. Daniel! Come and help me with this."

"Just a sec. We're at a boss."

My father sighs and shakes his head.

"Go enjoy yourselves, Jeannie." He smiles at Jensen. "You and I can continue our conversation later."

"Looking forward to it," Jensen says.

He and Katie follow me out onto the deck. I slide closed the patio door.

"Now what's wrong?" Jensen says.

Ugh. No.

I never told him about my encounter with Ilona at the mall. And I definitely don't want to bring it up right now.

"Nothing. I just...I'm nervous about everything. I don't know."

We descend the wooden steps and enter the backyard. I approach one of the several tables we set up for the party, and sit. A breeze blows past us, ruffling the paper tablecloths. In the distance, I can hear windchimes echo across the trees.

"Well, I have news, Genevieve." Katie sits beside me. "I already told Jensen, in the car. I couldn't wait."

"What is it?"

"You remember the code we found on the flash drive? The Word document that went along with Felyx's video?"

"Mhm." I hope I know what she's about to tell me.

"I figured it out!" she squeaks, and pulls out a piece of paper from her jean pocket. "It took me all week, but I got it." She lays the paper down in front of me.

It's covered in her scribbles.

$$A = 1 \times 4 + F = 1 \times 3$$

$$A = 1, \text{ so}$$

$A = 1$ $B = 2$, $C = 3$, $D = 4$, $E = 5$, $F = 6$, $G = 7$, $H = 8$, $I = 9$, $J = 10$, $K = 11$, $L = 12$, $M = 13$, $N = 14$, $O = 15$, $P = 16$, $Q = 17$, $R = 18$, $S = 19$, $T = 20$, $U = 21$, $V = 22$, $W = 23$, $X = 24$, $Y = 25$, $Z = 26$

But then what about F?

$$F = 1 ?$$

$F = 1$, $G = 2$, $H = 3$, $I = 4$, $J = 5$, $K = 6$, $L = 7$, $M = 8$, $N = 9$, $O = 10$, $P = 11$, $Q = 12$, $R = 13$, $S = 14$, $T = 15$, $U = 16$, $V = 17$, $W = 18$, $X = 19$, $Y = 20$, $Z = 21$, $A = 22$, $B = 23$, $C = 24$, $D = 25$, $E = 26$

4

5

9

14

17

6

23

And if A = 1×4, then the first 4
numbers are 4, 5, 9, 14, which
correlates to D, E, I, N
And if F = 1×3, then the last 3
numbers are 17, 6, 23, which
correlates to V, K, B.
D, E, I, N, V, K B ?
Felyx's last line is written: 5 2 6 -
7 3 4 1, which if the letters are put
into that order:
V, E, K - B, I, N, D
VEK BIND...
Vek'bind! He wants us to know
about Vek'bind!

"The letters and numbers correlate. So *here*," she points to the paper," he means A is equivalent to one. So the pattern would continue—B means two, and C means three, and so on. Same with this next part. But instead he shifts it so that F equals one, until you go through the alphabet consecutively and end on E. He wants you to use the A to start for the first four numbers he wrote, and the F for the last three numbers. The letters he leaves are *these*." She moves her finger to the corresponding spot on the sheet. "And if you put them in order of the numbers he arranged at the end, it spells *Vek'bind*, the Jintüroo's capital city!"

My heart skips a beat. Ilona's words resonate through my head. *Find Ira of the Jintüroo.*

"What...then, I mean, why would he want us to know that?"

"That's what we have to figure out." Jensen sighs. "There's another code on the document, but Katie hasn't been able to get that one yet. Right?"

"Yeah." She huffs. "It just isn't making sense to me. I don't think it follows the same algorithm as this first part."

"So..." I hand the paper back to Katie, "...we go to Vek'bind. And we figure out what Felyx wanted us to know."

"Genevieve, that isn't—"

"Hey, guys." Floyd opens the backyard gate, wearing a shirt with the periodic table of elements on it. "I hope I'm not too early. I brought...cookies." He smiles, holding out a box of baked goods. "Hi, Katie." His grin widens at her name.

He approaches her and kisses her on the cheek.

"Hey." Her cheeks are rosy red. "I'm glad you were able to make it."

"We finished our group project early. Where should I put these, Genevieve?" He motions to the cookies.

"Oh, they can go inside." I point to the patio door. "Go set them down and grab something to drink."

"Sounds good. Be back in a few."

When he's far enough away from us, I turn to Jensen and Katie.

"We know now that my mother isn't dead, right?" I look to Jensen. "If the letter you told us about—that Mengurion Maldridge wrote to the Council—is true, then we know the Binding Spell locked her away in the Void King's body. We need to find a way to get her back."

"But we don't even know if that's going to help," Jensen says. "For all we know, Felyx could be talking about something completely different."

"Katie already made a good point that the Binding Spell seems related to the Jintüroo's magic. It can't be coincidence that Felyx mentioned it, too."

"I agree with Genevieve," Katie says. "Maybe they can tell us more about Isaac Banewind. Honestly, *anything* would be useful to know."

"Yeah, you're right," Jensen says. "But I think we should at least wait until my family comes, and we figure out what the Council is going to do to help us. Does that sound good?"

"I like that plan," I say. "And maybe, in the meantime, you can teach me how the heck to work my powers."

I love the end of summer. The weather is still warm, but by night you can tell the wind's breeze has cooled. There is a unique smell to the air, with that humid woodsy musk giving way to the faintest hint of autumn leaves. It's crisp and fresh, calm and stable. It brings with it an exciting horizon of opportunity, from Halloween to Thanksgiving to Christmas to New Years. Although signifying the summer's end, it is, in many ways, the beginning of everything that makes the year exciting. And Labor Day marks the start of this transition.

As the party continues, soon the evening has blanketed the backyard. The music dances through the air from our outdoor stereo system, and the stringed lights hanging from the tree branches twinkle like hundreds of fireflies above the guests. Laughter and banter mix in beautiful harmony, as the food slowly disappears and the guests' waistlines expand.

I'm sitting at our table, next to Jensen, with my head resting on his shoulder. Katie and Floyd are leaning into each other, smiling, chatting, and enjoying the tranquility that is this moment. Something I wish could last forever.

Something I'm scared will disappear.

Jensen's cell phone rings.

"Hello?"

I watch his face, hoping to get a sense of who he may be talking to. He looks at me as he stands from his chair. His face remains expressionless.

One second, he mouths, a finger raised to signal me. He turns away and heads towards the house.

"Who do you think that is?" Katie looks over her shoulder, at Jensen.

I shrug. "Maybe Sadie? I don't know."

My phone vibrates, and I see a text from Jensen.

Come out front.

"I'll be right back," I say to Katie and Floyd. "Does anyone need anything?"

"Nope, I'm good. Thanks, Jeannie." Floyd is playing with Katie's braids.

She giggles as I proceed around the house, to the front yard.

Jensen is standing on the porch. And Kingston Starmantle is sitting on the stairs next to him. The color drains from my face, as the apparition of the pit in my stomach sucks away the rest of my body's energy.

"Hello, Genevieve." Kingston stands, watching me approach. "Nice to see you again."

I'm caught off-guard by his appearance. And I don't just mean his presence. Yes, that he is here at my home is startling in itself. But what I'm more intrigued by is that he looks so...normal. He's wearing a pair of boat shoes and bright-colored shorts, with a polo. The only thing he's missing to complete the yuppie-boy ensemble is a sweater tied around his neck and a pair of aviator sunglasses. His shoulders are broad, but he's slender, and his body tapers down into a V-shape at his waist. His white hair remains styled, with just a few loose strands dangling over his forehead. There's not an ounce of armor to his name.

"Kingston came here to give you something." Jensen eyes him suspiciously. "At least, that's what he's telling me."

Kingston frowns. "Yes, that's exactly what I'm doing. Can I have a moment alone with Genevieve?"

"What? Are you serious? You think—"

"It's okay, Jensen." I touch his shoulder. "I'll meet you in the backyard."

He looks from Kingston to me, and sighs. "Scream if you have to." He glares at Kingston before opening the front door.

I wait for it to close.

"Why did you kill Scythe!" I pound Kingston on the chest. "You stabbed him!" *Punch.* "You let him die." *Punch, punch.* "You hurt him!" *Punch, punch, punch.*

"Hey, hey! Stop it." He tries to grab my fists. "Genevieve, stop it."

My breathing is rapid, hollow. I shudder and step back from him.

"He isn't dead, remember? You brought him back. He's fine."

"But what if I hadn't? What if I couldn't?"

"But you did. And I know that doesn't make what I did right. But Genevieve..." Kingston sighs, "...I knew he wouldn't die. I knew you'd be able to bring him back. That was the plan all along."

"Wha-what?"

Kingston reaches into his pocket and pulls out a folded letter.

"Here." He hands it to me. "Read it."

I hesitate before grabbing it from him. I recognize

Scythe's handwriting.

> Genevieve,
>
> I hope you're doing okay. I am so sorry for everything you're going through. I wish it were different.
>
> Please don't be mad at Kingston. It isn't his fault. He did the right thing. It needed to be done.
>
> Magister Maldridge knew the plan would work. I never told you because he had asked me not to, but Kingston was the one who gave me your mother's note and necklace after Maldridge told him where to find them. I know this doesn't make a lot of sense, but one day you'll know more.
>
> Stay safe. Don't die.
>
> —Scythe

"What the hell is this?" White-hot anger boils deep inside me. "Scythe gave this to you?"

"He thought it would help."

I laugh. "Help what? Your guilty conscience for sticking a sword through his stomach? Perfect. Glad you can feel better about that." I stare at the paper again. "I don't even know what to say."

"Yeah, well, I don't either." Kingston reaches down to his side. "I also came to give you this." He hands me a bubblegum-pink gift bag.

On the side of it is a logo of a white heart with bold magenta letters that say, *P.J.'s*, stamped in the middle of it. Below it is a lip print shimmering with tie-dyed colors, as if someone kissed the bag. Spilling over the top is purple tissue paper, embedded with glitter and sparkles.

"Happy Birthday," Kingston says, in a gruff tone.

"It isn't my birthday."

"Trying to be funny." He sighs.

I push through the tissue paper, reaching in to grab the contents. I pull out a rectangular box, its color matching that of the bag.

"It's a portal key," Kingston says, as I open it.

The octahedral crystal is opaque lavender, dangling from a gold keychain.

"It was made special for you. Requested by Mengurion Maldridge. It has a pre-determined, permanent location loaded onto it. But you can't get to it yet, as the portal to wherever it goes isn't functioning. And no, I don't know where that is. I just told them I would make sure you got it. And here." He hands me a photo. "The magister also wanted you to have this. The last favor I'm doing for a while." He brushes past me and starts to walk away.

"Wait!" I turn around and grab his arm.

He pauses in mid-stance, rigid as he looks back at me. I stand there in silence, unsure of what to say, so he keeps on walking.

"Oh, one more thing," he calls to me, from the sidewalk. "Can you send Nick home?"

"Huh?"

"You know...Nick. Your neighbor."

"Danny's friend?"

"Yeah. I've been the babysitter for the last few weeks. Surprise."

I'm lucky I don't break my jaw at the speed it falls open.

"You've been watched and protected by more people

than you know, Genevieve." He turns his back to me and continues down the sidewalk. "I told you, I'm done with favors."

"You...were *you* involved in my brother being taken by the Magician?"

My heart is racing, and my nostrils flare as that seething anger boils up in my soul once more.

"It's in the past, Genevieve. Good night."

I shove the portal key back into the bag and swing open the front door. I slam it shut with such ferocity that the Labor Day wreath hanging on the outside clamors to the ground.

After I catch my breath, I look down at the photo Kingston gave me, and my eyes widen in disbelief. I rush outside to the table and slam the photo down in front of Jensen and Katie. They jump, startled by the sound.

"What is this?" Jensen picks up the photo.

His eyes flash with befuddlement.

"Exactly." My voice tremors. "What is *this*?"

As Katie leans over to see the photo, she gasps.

"What is it?" Floyd also looks at the photo. "Who are those people?"

As the table's candlelight flickers across the picture, I see my mother smiling back at me, a joyous look spread across her face. She wears a beautiful silver cloak, and her golden pendant hangs around her neck. She's standing in the center of a group of people. To her right stands my uncle, Felyx Crimsley, raising a glass in a toast, his eyes creased from laughter. His arm is wrapped around a woman's waist, squeezing her to his side. Her silver hair cascades down her face, her green lips pulled into a vibrant smile—something I'm not used to seeing on Valkryn Salharia.

And to my mother's left, wearing a bold crimson

cloak, is the Magician. His face is clean-shaven, his hair styled back, and he also holds a woman that I don't recognize, resting her head upon his chest while raising a glass into the air.

"Wait. I recognize that one." Floyd points to another woman kneeling on the floor next to my mother, holding out her glass. "Isn't that your teacher?"

Sadie Hawthorne's face smiles back at us, clinking glasses with a woman kneeling on my mother's other side.

A breeze flows through the backyard, extinguishing the candle's flame and the people's faces along with it.

Victor DeWinter places the last of the trash bags onto the tree lawn. The recycling container and garbage can have already been pulled down to the corner of the driveway, but the remnants of the party are too much to fit into the receptacles alone. He stacks the black bags against each other, brushing the dirt from his hands as he heads back up toward the house. He pauses at the top of the driveway, leaning his backside against Genevieve's Honda Civic.

He lets out a long sigh before reaching into his shirt pocket and pulling out a cigar. He runs the dark brown paper under his nose as he breathes in the sweet, tarry smell that has been an ongoing vice of his for decades. It's late now, almost midnight, and Genevieve and Daniel have been in bed for a while, not a sound emerging from upstairs as he cleaned up the remainder of the kitchen and backyard.

I deserve this. He nods as he pulls out the lighter from his pants pocket. *A cigar every now and then won't kill me. Especially to celebrate the successful end to Labor Day.*

Cheers to the end of summer.

He cups the cigar around his hand as he sparks the lighter, rolling the cigar's end in the ember flames. The pulsating glow brightens with each puff he takes, a stark contrast to the darkness that lines the neighborhood. The black smoke circles around him now, and he closes his eyes as he breathes deeply, lost in the moment of bliss.

Cracckkkkkkk!

The snapping noise forces Victor to open his eyes. An astonished look spreads across his face as he sees the end of his cigar snap, crackle, and fizzle. The fiery glow is snuffed out as suddenly as it had emerged, and a chill crawls down his fingertips and into his hand. His eyes grow wide as he pulls the cigar closer to him, lifting his glasses to examine the tip, which is now frozen solid and covered in ice.

"Addisyn would kill you if she saw you smoking one of those cancer sticks, you know." Sadie Hawthorne's voice breaks through the night's air. "One of the rare things she was never fond of about you."

Her heels reverberate past Victor, ricocheting between the sides of the houses. She approaches him, with her palms clasped in front of her, resting at her waist. The moonlight catches off the golden strands of her hair.

"Sarah..." Victor steps closer to her.

A forlorn smile spreads across her face. "Nobody's used my formal name for a long time. It sounds so unfamiliar."

"Genevieve said you were back. I never thought I'd see you again."

"I promised Addisyn that I...that *we* would not continue down the path we were taking. You know as well as I do it was becoming too dangerous. We were passing boundaries we shouldn't have approached long before that. She was my best friend, Victor. You guys had a family." She shakes her head. "We couldn't go on the way we were. Even after she was gone."

Victor stands inches from her. He takes the back of his hand and brushes it down the side of her face, and stops at her chin, where he places her face between his fingers. She closes her eyes and nuzzles her head into his hand, letting his fingertips touch between her lips.

"It is so good to see you," Victor whispers, his eyes misty behind his glasses. "It is so, so good."

Sadie opens her eyes and pulls away, breaking the trance between them.

"Victor." She straightens and puts her hair back behind her ear. "Victor, it is good to see you, too. But I did not come to pick up the pieces of a fractured fantasy. Believe me, if it weren't absolutely necessary, you would still think me gone."

"What is it?"

"Let's go inside to talk. I think we need to sit down."

26

ONE THOUSAND

MIRRORS

"IT'S BEAUTIFUL," SCYTHE WHISPERS, staring in awe at the endless sea.

The undulating waves dance across the surface, carrying their blue essence far into the stretching horizon. High above, the seabirds cast down their shadows as they swoop through the briny air, singing the harbor's melody.

Maldridge's eyes crease as he smiles at Scythe.

"You are not the first to be mesmerized by the aquatic beauty of Gardonia, my dear boy. It is known as the City of One Thousand Mirrors for good reason." He inhales deeply. "They say, at times, the sun's reflection off the crystal-clear waters occurs with such intensity that many a sailor have been blinded by the light. But in exchange, they are entranced with an eternal peace."

"What is that?" Scythe points at a figure's outline barely distinguishable on the horizon.

"Ah, yes." Maldridge nods. "The Coral Palace. A place you frequented quite often in your youth."

Scythe sighs in frustration. "I don't remember." He pounds his fist against the balcony's marble rail, gazing over the top at the rocky shores far below. "I don't remember any of it."

"In time. You must be patient."

The sound of footsteps nearing rings through the open air as a woman emerges from the balcony's golden alcove.

"I'm sorry to keep you waiting." She moves toward the large, round table.

On its top is an extravagant spread of fruits, meats, and other delicacies. The chalices and cutlery sparkle in the sun's rays.

"Please." She gestures to the chairs across from her.

Scythe and Maldridge take their seats.

"It's wonderful to see you again, Mengurion. It's been too long." She flashes a white smile, which is a stark contrast to her onyx skin.

She rests her hand against her cheek, causing the row of golden bangles to slide further down her arm.

"Tell me, has our hospitality been to your liking?"

"As always, it is exemplary but unnecessary, Emora. Your generosity is too kind." Maldridge picks up a long-stemmed pipe from the table and runs his fingers underneath the bowl until a cherry-scented billow is rising from the chamber.

Emora looks to Scythe. "And how are you doing?"

Her golden hood flutters in the breeze as the rest of her robes knocks against the table, keeping in rhythm with the distant windchimes.

"Okay, I guess," Scythe replies.

The turquoise robe he wears is uncomfortable to him, like an unfamiliar touch. Strangling.

"Fair," she says. "I can only imagine how challenging this is for you."

"Maldridge told me that you're the one who put the original hex on me." Scythe's words are curt, with an underlying hostility to them. "That true?"

Emora leans forward, and the pearl necklace she wears scrapes against the porcelain plate in front of her.

"It is, yes."

"And because of that, I remember *nothing* about my childhood," he hisses, clenching his fists.

Maldridge rests his aged hand against Scythe's arm.

"It's all right." Emora nods at Maldridge. "His hostility is justified. I would be just as angry, given the circumstances. In truth, what right did I have to deprive him of his memories, his past existence?" She leans back in her chair. "For that, I am sorry. I truly am. At the same time, it had to be done. To protect you. And your parents knew that when they asked me. I would do it all again."

"I don't even remember my parents," Scythe whispers, his voice catching in his throat.

He sees his face's reflection in the silver plate, the bruises and cuts almost healed.

"I don't remember...anything."

"But you will," Emora says. "The hex was broken when Kingston stabbed you. The memories will slowly return."

"And what now?" Scythe looks from Emora to Maldridge. "What am I supposed to do?"

"Prepare," says a gruff, stoutly voice. "And pray we aren't too late."

Dorndrick Wolfshire emerges onto the balcony, his silver armor radiating with the sun's splendor.

"Emora. Mengurion. Good to see you." He

approaches the table, but stands with his arms folded, staring at Scythe. "So this is him?"

Emora smiles at Scythe, nodding. "It is, indeed."

"Prove it."

"I'm sorry?" Scythe furrows his eyebrows. "Look, I don't know what you think—"

"We don't have time to play petty games," Dorndrick says. "If you are who they say you are, and I'm going to be risking my life protecting you, I need proof. It's that simple. The Void King is very much alive, and even at his weakest right now, I barely survived the encounter. If he returns to his true form...please." His voice softens. "Just show me."

Scythe sighs as he stands from his chair. He turns to the brazier burning in the corner of the balcony. He holds out his hand, and the ember coals sputter out as the basin becomes bathed in a chilled frost. The hissing steam rises high and disappears into the blue sky.

Dorndrick's gaze remains glued to the brazier.

Scythe exhales deeply as he turns his hand around, raising it into the air. As he does so, the frost-bitten basin begins to thaw out, with several crackles popping sporadically within. The damp coals awaken with a red glow as a spark ignites them into a fiery inferno. Within moments, the brazier is alight again, its flames burning more ferociously than before. The black soot is carried high into the sky, with the wind scattering it off the balcony and towards the vast sea.

Maldridge grins as he bites down on his pipe, staring at the burning flames.

"There." Scythe falls back into his chair. "Happy?"

Dorndrick nods to Emora. "I will let them know that what you say is true." He turns and looks at Scythe. "That Isaac Banewind, the last surviving member of the

Banewind lineage, the Royal Family of Formulists with the power to dual-wield Fire and Ice...is alive."

"I think I prefer to be called Scythe." He averts his gaze from Dorndrick.

A nearby ship's horn drowns out his words.

END OF BOOK ONE

ABOUT THE AUTHOR

Matt Chapman grew up
outside of Cleveland and
now lives in St. Louis,
Missouri where he is
completing his residency
in Psychiatric medicine at
Washington University in
St. Louis. He is a graduate
of Creighton University
School of Medicine where
he obtained his MD and a
graduate of Saint Louis
University where he
majored in Biology.

Matt has had a passion for writing and reading since
childhood and continues to find time for these interests
among his other pursuits, including medical education
and leadership studies. He is currently working on his next
novel in *The Banewind Series*.

Connect with Matt online:
Facebook: mbchapman90
Instagram: @banewind_series
Snapchat: @banewind_series
Twitter: @mbchapman90

CPSIA information can be obtained
at www.ICGtesting.com
Printed in the USA
LVHW111432171120
671938LV00033B/312

9 781611 533941